Full Circle:
The Rami Johnson Story

Books by C. Everard Palmer

The Cloud with the Silver Lining
Big Doc Bitteroot
The Sun Salutes You
The Hummingbird People
The Wooing of Beppo Tate
My Father, Sun-Sun Johnson
Full Circle: The Rami Johnson Story
Baba and Mr Big
A Dog Called Houdini
A Cow Called Boy

Full Circle:
The Rami Johnson Story

C. Everard Palmer

MACMILLAN
CARIBBEAN

Macmillan Education
Between Towns Road, Oxford OX4 3PP
A division of Macmillan Publishers Limited
Companies and representatives throughout the world

www.macmillan-caribbean.com

ISBN 1-4050-1366-4 (hardback)
ISBN 0-333-99648-8 (paperback)

Text © C. Everard Palmer 2003
Design and illustration © Macmillan Publishers Limited 2003

First published 2003

All rights reserved; no part of this publication may be reproduced, stored in a retrieval system, transmitted in any form or by any means, electronic, mechanical, photocopying, recording, or otherwise, without the prior written permission of the publishers.

Designed by Wendy Bann
Typeset by EXPO Holdings, Malaysia
Cover design by Gary Fielder, AC Design
Cover illustration by Judy Ann Macmillan

Printed and bound in Malaysia

2007 2006 2005 2004 2003
10 9 8 7 6 5 4 3 2 1

Contents

1	Sun-Sun Johnson	9
2	A pleasant visit	13
3	Crayfish soup	20
4	Memorial	26
5	Yam hills, curry goat and folk songs	31
6	Donna Rae	39
7	Jake Hibbertson	45
8	Christmas	50
9	Cripes Randall	59
10	Staying on at River Bottom	65
11	'No man is an Island'	72
12	Making progress	78
13	The garden party	83
14	Harvest	88
15	Hit the road, Jake	94
16	Examinations	98
17	Harvest Sunday	103
18	Cripes comes of age	110
19	Interlude	114
20	Two graduations and a wedding	118
21	Full circle	122

Dedication

To the people of Kendal District, Hanover, where I grew up and experienced the joys and sorrows of rural life in Jamaica

No man is an *Iland*, intire of it selfe; every
man is a peece of the *Continent*, a part of the
maine; … any mans *death* diminishes *me*,
because I am involved in *Mankinde*; And therefore
never send to know for whom the *bell* tolls;
It tolls for *thee*.

John Donne

1

Sun-Sun Johnson

At my father's funeral, my mother asked me: 'Rami, what are you going to do now?'

My answer was: 'Why, plant yams, of course.' And that was exactly what I intended to do, and more.

But for those of you who do not know the story, *My Father, Sun-Sun Johnson*, let me give you a brief account. I'll start at the beginning.

My father, Sun-Sun Johnson, was a businessman and farmer, and a successful one, too. He planted yams and bananas, a lot of both. He also reared a few animals: some cows and a few mules that were kept as draught animals. And he prospered. He was an easygoing man, a kind man, but, as he mellowed with age, he became careless. He allowed people to take advantage of him. He lent money on a handshake and a smile. He allowed people to harvest mangoes and sell them in the market at a profit without charging a fee for the privilege. Nothing was really wrong with this latter kindness of his because it was far better to let those who were in need benefit than having the mangoes rot on the ground.

My father had a rival in Jake Hibbertson, another small-time businessman, but a rapacious one. He saw through my father's weakness and used this knowledge to chip away at his success.

He approached Father with one cock-and-bull story after another, stories of need. This relative who lived in another part of the island was sick and needed expensive surgery. Oh, and he had lost money on a speculative scheme and needed an instant cash injection to pay off a debt. Could Father help? Any story to get a loan. In his cunning, Jake used these monies to purchase lands, lot by lot. He even opened a store.

So Jake came up fast, and my father began to decline. When his truck was involved in an accident and he was at fault, my father lost in a big way, even losing the truck.

Have you noticed that when things begin to go wrong in one's life they just get worse? Murphy's Law of, course. And when an animal is wounded, how predators go on the attack! So it was with my father.

Thieves began to raid his banana fields and harvest some of his fruit before he could. They even managed to steal two of his cows, and the word was they were sold to a butcher in another district.

In an attempt to recover some of his losses, he began to gamble. But, as everyone knows, when someone is desperate to win, the last thing he should do is gamble. His chances of winning are just about nil. Mark you, my father did not get too deep into this last vice, but his losses were enough to make him more desperate.

This led him to Jake Hibbertson, the man he had once lent money to. Now he was the borrower, and Jake drove a hard bargain. Jake demanded not interest but collateral – the deed to our beloved Robin Hill, a choice piece of hilltop land on which our house was built. The land was called Robin Hill and so was the house, a magnificent structure that commanded a view of our small town. It exuded comfort: four bedrooms, sitting rooms, a den, a library, a large kitchen and a dining room. Attached to it by a covered walkway were the maid's quarters. And all this went to Jake when Father couldn't pay back the loan on time and Jake foreclosed.

My mother had already left. When Father's handling of his affairs became so erratic, she obtained a legal separation.

Maybe she meant only to give Father a kick in the pants so he would correct his ways. But with the loss of Robin Hill the separation quickly turned into a divorce.

Brad and Arlene, my younger siblings, went to live with her; I chose to stick with Father.

We moved to the last parcel of land – he called it River Bottom – a fertile acreage, never planted by him. On this land was a small house, a shack compared to Robin Hill, but it was home. We settled in.

In my father's eyes there was a light like a beacon that expressed both sorrow and determination, two emotions concocted in the cauldron of his anguished soul. In the days that followed his loss of not only Robin Hill but also his wife, he spoke very little, a man who had got his name Sun-Sun because of his rich humour, easygoing manner and goodwill. I knew how he felt. I could feel his pain. He had climbed the ladder of success and had come tumbling down, and now he had to start all over again. I knew that this time he meant to stay atop the ladder, not *if* he reached it, but *when* he reached it.

But more misfortune was in store for us. Not satisfied with wresting Robin Hill from Father, Jake began to court Ma. Father took the news with gritted teeth, but I was broken up. How could he? How could she?

I think she was so angry at Father's failure that she did it out of sheer spite, because such a union just didn't make sense. Boy, was I happy I had stuck with Father! How could I stand living under the same roof as the man who had ruined him?

After Ma's divorce was final, she and Jake were married. She, Arlene and Brad moved back into Robin Hill. Jake's destruction of my father was complete.

Father suffered in silence, but he did not let it deter him in his quest for climbing the ladder once again. He planted yams, he reaped bananas from the rich soil, big bunches of them. Things were looking just dandy when one night a fire broke out at Robin Hill, and my father and I raced up there. After all Arlene and Brad were there; Ma was there.

Father got there first, and I was just in time to see him rush into the burning building, bringing out Ma and her baby by Jake, and the children next, and going in one more time to rescue Jake. He managed to rescue him all right, throwing him out of a window, but he didn't make it back outside. He perished in the flames. Hence the funeral. Hence my mother's question and hence my answer: 'Why, plant yams, of course.' To finish what my father had begun – taking my place on the ladder, climbing it rung by slippery rung, and staying on it.

2

A pleasant visit

Ma had managed to rent a vacant house from Mr Stanfield Willet, who was on a two-year visit to his daughter in Philadelphia, USA. Ma was once again an estranged wife. She had begun to see the error of her ways. She had divorced a good man who, true to his nature, had given his life in an effort to save an enemy. It seemed that her love for Father had never really died, not entirely, but had been in some sort of remission. With the tragedy, it returned, so to speak, and her disgust of Jake began.

Jake, who had suffered minor burns, was recovering and had taken up residence again on the second storey of his store. He had had a house which he had put up for sale after he moved into Robin Hill, and unlucky for him it had been sold to Mrs Hilcher. So it was back to living above his store, back almost to where he had started. For him, too, the estrangement was a bitter pill to swallow. His wife had left him. Such a thing should not have happened to Jake Hibbertson. Normally it was *he* who would do the leaving. He was a pillar, the town's new kingpin, the man who had risen from obscurity to take away the throne from Sun-Sun Johnson, to take his prized home and then his wife. And now he had lost both, and more – he had lost an heir, for Ma's baby by Jake died soon after the fire. Whether it was from smoke inhalation or complications arising from it, the baby wasted away and died. An autopsy was inconclusive. Jake was bitter.

He showed no remorse for my father's death. It had been Sun-Sun's weakness that had caused his death, he told someone who dared to upbraid him for doing what he had done to my father. Always giving when giving was foolhardy. The martyred fool, as he called him. With these comments Jake consoled himself.

The deaths of Father and the baby were not the only ones in our family. Max, my pup, had been killed when he chased a mongoose across the road and was hit by a car. I buried him in the backyard, buried him with some bones he had contended with but had not wholly discarded.

I was living in the small cottage at River Bottom, alone. Its exterior bore a shabby look, but inside it was clean and comfortable. The kitchen was a shed no more than six feet from the cottage, and, before he died, Father had built a covered walk that connected them.

At the end of my first week in the cottage, Ma brought Brad and Arlene for a visit. Ma carried flowers for Father's grave. She placed them at the head of the grave, and the four of us stood there solemnly for a minute just looking at the simple wooden cross that marked it.

'In time I will give it a proper headstone,' I said.

She looked at me, smiling. 'I know you will.'

There were circles under her eyes and she was a few pounds lighter. She had lost so much and in so short a time – my father, her old ex, Jake, now her new ex, and the baby. But she looked great. My mother always looked great.

Arlene and Brad went to explore the cottage. So did Ma, after a little while. I followed them, from time to time throwing cold water on Ma's 'Oh my Gods' each time she saw something she considered substandard. She shook my bed and it rocked gently like a cradle.

'This rickety bed!'

'It will do for now, Ma.'

'And no bathroom?'

'The river's my bathroom. It runs right outside my door. The latrine's out back.'

Inside the bedroom was a washstand equipped with a jug for fetching and holding water and a washbasin where I washed my face and brushed my teeth.

'Rami, I don't like this. You can't stay here. Move in with us. We have enough room. Three bedrooms. You could bunk with Brad. You know how much he'd like that.'

'Yes!' from Brad. Eyeing me, he asked, 'Will you?'

I winked at him. 'Not right now, Brad.'

'Do consider, Rami. I'm worried for you.' Ma was coaxing, not strong-arming. In the blink of an eye she had lost two men in her life. She was afraid of losing another, but she was leaving it up to me to choose to move in with them. She was genuinely afraid for me, and I appreciated the concern. She was a mother. I was still her son, a teenager, but to her still a boy.

'I have a mission, Ma. Let me see it through. I'll be careful. And apart from being lonely, what can happen to me?'

'I don't like it one bit. Down here in this hole at night, all by yourself. And what about school?' she argued. 'Since your father died you haven't been to school. I've waited this long to ask you about that. Do you think he wanted you to give up your education?'

'That's where you're wrong, Ma. I'm not giving that up. It's merely a hiatus, a break. And not entirely a break. I may not be in school in body, but I haven't really left. I'm going to study for the GCE exams. Fortunately I don't have to be in school to do that. And here's the good thing – you being a teacher you can help me with English. You teach English, so you see it will work out just fine. I've begun puttering around in Geography and History. I've always done well in those subjects. I'll be doing them at Advanced Level, along with British Constitution.'

She was smiling at me. 'You have everything planned out, haven't you?' She was coming around. She was a strong believer in a good education. So long as I was keeping my hand in, she was pleased.

When she married Jake, she had given up her teaching job at the High School, but after the debacles of the fire, the two deaths in the family and the estrangement from Jake, she had re-entered the profession.

'Are you eating well?' she asked with a mother's concern. 'Of course not,' she answered her question herself. 'Come up for dinner as often as you want. I don't like the idea of your cooking for yourself. Jeez, Rami, you're only seventeen! You're not old enough to be on your own. I'll send Fantasia down with dinners and to help out.'

Fantasia was her maid.

'Ma, it means I'll have to grow up fast. Trust me, Ma. I told you I was going to plant yams and that's what I'm going to do. Yams and bananas. I'm going to finish what Father started. He had fallen down, but he was getting up again. He began here, and here I'll stay to finish what he had in mind. I intend to see that hillside . . .' I made a sweeping motion with my arm. '. . . that hillside out there covered with yams and bananas. And as they climb towards town, . . .' Our village was growing so fast I used to refer to it as a town – narrator's licence. '. . . I will march with the fields right back up there, and I vow to get Robin Hill back in the family's possession. And I'll finish my education, too. OK with you? I'll do the entire thing in about five years. Don't talk me out of it. You can't. You mustn't try. Some beef soup while you're here?' I pointed towards the kitchen.

She smiled. 'Why not? I brought you some ackees. Do you have any codfish?'

'Right here in the cupboard, Ma.'

'You are your father's son,' she said. 'That was how he was in the old days. Full of fight.' Then she saw Brad and Arlene down by the river. She called to them: 'Children, be careful.' To me she said: 'You may cook the ackees and codfish another day. But let's see what your soup looks like.' She opened the pot and had to crinkle her eyes against the steam that rose up in her face. 'This soup needs to be rescued,' she said. 'No aroma.' Then, like a doctor during surgery, she called for condiments: 'Scallion, thyme, black pepper . . .' She tasted the soup. 'A pinch more salt, too.'

I had scallion and salt, but none of the others.

'Boy,' she said, 'how do you expect to make a good meal without having even the basics?'

'I'll learn,' I shot back.

'Very well,' she said, standing with arms akimbo, 'I'll have to stock your larder with some necessary ingredients.'

That was OK with me. I stepped outside the kitchen. Brad and Arlene were stooping by the river bank, reaching into the water. Presently they came running up the slope.

'There are crayfish in there,' Brad sang out. 'I saw them.'

'We were trying to catch them, but they were too quick,' Arlene joined in. 'They darted away backwards and forwards, quick as a flash.'

'Tell you what, you two. One Saturday I'll come and get you, and I'll show you how to catch them. How is that for a promise?'

'Will you really?' Brad said elatedly.

'I sure will.'

'Ma, you heard that?' Arlene asked.

'Yes, I heard. You can visit your brother any time, but be careful around water.' Coming out of the kitchen Ma turned to me. 'Rami, come up for dinner tomorrow. Promise?'

Sunday dinners were always special. Rice-and-peas with roast beef, or chicken done one of several ways, sometimes steamed snapper or kingfish, sometimes lobster. And there were so many variations to dessert – like corn pone, soursop drink, papaya or pineapple slices – I wasn't about to miss out on that.

'Sure, Ma. I'll be there after church. So long as Jake won't be there.'

'We're through, Rami. Jake's an evil man. He only married me to hurt your father more than he already had. He isn't even penitent for his death. The man died to save his life, and he has shown no remorse whatsoever. D'you know he has accused your father of setting the fire?'

'What? How low can that man go?'

'That's not all, Rami. He accused me too – for the baby's death. He said I killed the baby to get rid of him.'

'My God! Is there no limit to his evil?'

'I have to admit now, Rami, my shame for how I treated your father. I ran out on him at the first sign of trouble. My hands aren't clean, either. I look back now and question my intentions at the time I married Jake.'

'Thanks for saying that, Ma. I never doubted that you loved Father. I'll be there tomorrow.'

We had our beef soup, which, with Ma's intervention, tasted quite good.

'I'll do what I can to help with your GCE studies, but, young man, you'll need more help than I can give. I'll speak to Mr Dumfries of the Geography department and to Mrs Quill of History. They're friends of mine. I think they'll be happy to guide you in your studies in those areas. This is a positive move on your part, doing the GCE. Getting an education is good, for if one fails in one's plans and loses one's fortunes, one will still have one's education. That is something solid to fall back on. Let me take your prospectus with me. Tomorrow when you come by, you can tell me what areas of study you've selected, and I'll get you some texts.' She looked out of the window. 'It's getting late,' she observed.

Down in the valley the shadows were assembling to herald in the dusk. We could still see sunlight licking at the hilltops and glinting on zinc roofs up in town, but down here it always arrives late and leaves early.

Arlene and Brad reminded me of my promise. 'Remember?' they said. 'The crayfish.'

'You bet,' I assured them.

'When?' Brad asked.

'Next Saturday,' I said.

Brad blew a wolf whistle – show off.

I walked them part of the way. It had been a very pleasant visit.

3

Crayfish soup

The next Saturday I went up and fetched Arlene and Brad. They were gung-ho, which was the spirit I expected.

In a way Ma had kept us sheltered from the real world. I was always envious of some of the town boys who ran freely, not getting into trouble but running free. How I should have liked to frolic in the rivers with them, damming the river in the dry season when the flow of water was down to a trickle and then baling most of the water out of the pool below to catch the crayfish left stranded there; then making crayfish soup, boiling it in a washed-out four-gallon can in which kerosene oil had been imported. I would have loved to be able to shinny up a tall coconut tree, sit in the crown of fronds and cut open a young coconut, jelly coconut to us, and drink the liquid it held; then scoop out the delicious flesh and eat it with brown sugar. Those boys had the best of outdoor living while we looked on from inside our cocoons.

But it was different now. I was out on my own, lord of my own designs, and now I had a chance to introduce my young siblings to my world.

'Take your shoes off,' I told them.

They complied, kicking their sneakers off.

'What now?' Brad asked.

'Let's go and kick some dew off some pretty grass.'

'Really?' they said as though they were twinned in speech.

They were sold. Their twinkling eyes and glittering teeth said as much.

We went up the hillside to where a swath of the softest grass grew. Bed grass we called it, because come summer it would be silky-brown from the sun, making for good mattress-filling for those people who could not afford store-bought bedding. But now there was a small sea of green, a pretty sight with the pinheads of silvery dew adorning the swath.

'Come on,' I urged. 'Walk, kick, get your feet wet.'

We kicked our way through the swath, destroying the pinheads of dew and bathing our feet in the process. From their giggling, I knew my sibs were on top of the world.

'It's such fun,' Arlene chortled.

'Cool,' Brad said. And that was not a figure of speech. Our feet were deliciously wet and cool. Under our feet the grass was bent down, but in a few minutes it would rear up again.

'Do you do this every morning, Rami?' Arlene asked.

'No, not really.'

'If I lived here, I'd do it every morning,' said Brad.

With that behind us we went to the river to catch some crayfish. I carried a basket woven from strips of bamboo. Arlene had a pail and Brad was armed with a stick. I set the basket in the water under the river bank with its open end facing upstream. Using his stick, Brad stirred up the water, driving the fish downstream and into the basket. When I lifted it, water streamed out of the basket, but the trapped crayfish were left jumping, trying unsuccessfully to escape. I scooped them out and into the pail that had enough water in it to keep the fish alive and in their environment.

Although her eyes had been sparkling a minute ago, Arlene was eyeing the fish with some trepidation.

'Some of them have claws, Rami,' she said. 'Will they bite?'

'Not really bite, Arlene. It would be more like a nip. No real hurt.'

'Still I won't let them bite or nip me.'

'Just don't put your hand in the pail,' Brad advised.

We continued to fish. Brad raked the water with his stick, and the crayfish evacuated their hiding places for my basket. We even caught a big one with menacing claws. In the local vernacular this species is known as a 'mountain', obviously because of its size. It was as huge as a small lobster. Arlene was visibly afraid of this one.

'This one will give more than a nip, Rami,' she said.

'Yes, it will, but not to worry. As Brad advised, keep your hand out of the pail.'

Next we caught a fat frog, but being a champion jumper it sprang out of the basket back to safety.

Boys have a love-in with critters like frogs, and Brad asked, 'If we catch another one, can I keep it?'

'Sure, Brad. If we are quick enough to grab it before it leaps back into the water.'

'I hate frogs,' Arlene avowed.

'Girls!' Brad criticized.

But instead of another frog, we netted a river eel. I threw it back.

'Was that a snake?' Arlene asked.

'No, just an eel.'

It was obvious she didn't like the idea of sharing the water with something that seemed to be a cousin to a snake. She couldn't hide her discomfort. She began stomping the water as though to ward off any eel that might venture near her.

'I want to get out of the water now,' she said soon after.

'Me too,' Brad said.

I looked into the pail. 'Well, we've got enough for a good pot of soup, anyway.'

This was a Saturday I wanted them to remember. I would cook the soup the way the boys, the outdoor kings, cooked it. Not in the kitchen, but outside in the yard under the mango tree.

I found three stones of equal height and set them close enough for the pot to sit on, but with spaces between them for the firewood. After I had lit the fire and put a pot of water on, I began to clean the crayfish, cutting off the heads and pulling the entrails out. Into the pot they went along with slices of breadfruit, yams and choyote quash, better known as cho-choes.

At the appropriate time I added scallion, a small tomato, salt and black pepper – Ma had come through with stocking my larder. We sat around the fire and inhaled the aroma of the soup.

'This is fun,' Brad said, stoking the fire and sucking in some aroma, 'isn't it, Arlene?'

'Wait till I tell the girls at school on Monday,' she said. 'Can we do it again, Rami?'

'Sure. Anytime, Sis.'

'I like that.'

'Like what?' Brad asked.

'When Rami calls me Sis,' Arlene explained.

'Give me a break,' Brad said.

'Jealous?' Arlene teased.

Alfred Roper came ambling by. As he swung his arms, the shiny blade of his well-honed machete glinted in the sun. He was in his late fifties, toughened by days in the sun, toiling for this farmer or that, a man good with his machete, clearing brush or reaping sugar cane or bananas. He lived with his wife in a small house on the outskirts of town. They had no children.

'Mornin', Rami,' he said, lifting the front of his cap high enough to scratch his forehead with a finger.

It was now afternoon, but since I didn't wish to correct him, I said, 'Morning, Alfred. What's cooking?'

'Is you doin' the cookin',' he said with a chuckle, 'not me. Your brot'er an' sister visitin' you, I see. Mornin', chil'ren,' he said.

'Hello,' they replied.

They had probably seen Alfred many times before, but not close enough to get a greeting from him. Maybe the blade of his so-sharp machete looked too menacing to them, or his withered appearance scared them, because they both began to drift away.

Arlene had been stealing glances towards Father's grave but seemed uncertain whether or not she wanted to get close to it. Like most children, she and Brad probably feared getting close to a grave without the security of an adult along. Rife in our town was the superstition that a grave meant a ghost was about. But now they were sauntering in that direction, holding hands for mutual support. Finally they reached it but stood a respectable six feet or so away. At the head of the grave the wooden cross still had a couple of wreaths hanging from it. The flowers that Ma had brought last week were withered but were also still there.

Arlene bent to pick marigold flowers, and when she had gathered enough, she began to throw them at the grave, but they weren't reaching their target. Again both she and Brad held hands and advanced closer, until Arlene was able to place the flowers on the grave. Then, no longer afraid, the two of them went off looking for other flowers, and returned with handfuls of lilies, hibiscus and Joseph's coat. They smothered the entire mound with flowers.

'Nice to see 'em payin' respec' to dere papa,' observed Alfred.

'Yes, Alfred, it's very thoughtful of them.'

Alfred and I had been talking business. He was clearing brush for me, and he assured me that in a few days it would be all done and the land ready for planting.

When Arlene and Brad ambled back, the soup was just about done. It had a slight pinkness to it, coloured by the crayfish. The aroma promised a tasty meal. I invited Alfred to stay for lunch, and the four of us sat under the tree and relished the soup.

At first Arlene was a bit squeamish about eating it. Perhaps she remembered the incident of the frog jumping out of the basket and back into the river, or the eel that slithered around in the basket. Perhaps, to her, those critters had been too close to the crayfish and something from them had rubbed off on the crayfish, and we all know how girls detest hopping or slithering things. But after the crayfish flavour had begun to fondle her taste buds, she soon dug in in earnest.

Even if I say so myself, it was a great soup.

'This is good,' Brad said from deep in his throat. 'Eating here under the tree. What can top this? Great. Just great.'

'And not having to sit up straight,' Arlene said.

'And we can slurp,' Brad suggested, and backed it up with a huge slurp.

'Look, Brad,' Arlene said, putting her bowl up to her lips and slurping down some soup.

Alfred was amused. 'The cat's not 'ere,' he said, 'so the mice havin' a free-for-all.'

I grinned at him. I liked the way my sibs were enjoying their day out with me.

We hadn't cooked all the crayfish. A few specimens had been put aside for the sibs to take home as mementoes of their visit. Arlene had hers in an empty butter pan, while Brad's swam around in a jug. He vowed he was going to start a fish farm. Kids.

Brad refused to wash the charcoal smudges he had picked up on one cheek. He treasured them as a man treasures his first moustache. To him it was a badge, a memento of his encounter with the bush.

4

Memorial

Arlene and Brad's visit to Father's grave was timely. The following day, Sunday, three weeks after his death, was the day of his memorial service.

We had morning rain, but the sun came out in the afternoon and dried up the wetness and made for a good outing. Droves of people came out to pay their last respects to a man who had once been the object of admiration, but who, in later life, had stumbled.

The church was decorated with lilies and poinciana. For this type of service the lilies were apt, but a splash of red was, too, because it signified the spirit of the man who had lived so colourful a life. Near the altar were three easels holding photographs showing various stages of his life: including one of him as a youth, dressed as a surplice boy in our church, and others showing him sitting behind the wheel of his truck, dressed in full khaki and pith helmet and riding a mule, surveying work being done by workers, accepting a roast chicken he had won in a shooting contest, and also one of him taken when he was a deacon of our church.

The church was full. I was told that Jake had driven by a couple of times, perhaps monitoring the number of people attending, or perhaps wondering if it was safe for him to attend.

Arlene and Brad marched up the aisle and lit the candles.

The service began with a prayer by the Reverend Ledbetter, followed by Arlene and Brad reading aloud alternate verses from the Scriptures.

Then the Reverend gave the word, and the organist struck up the hymn 'Rock of Ages Cleft for Me'. A rather sad song, but we all joined in. Then Mrs Alicia Sugarman, lead singer of the choir, sweetened things up with Father's favourite tune, 'Sentimental Journey'. The honey-sweet voice and the peal of the organ had the desired effect, and the congregation joined in and rocked. It was heady, very heady, but it was appropriate and almost divine.

It was then time for those who knew Father to present vignettes of his life. First, Mr Talbot, another landowner, took the podium. His story was about his and Father's trip to Kingston, their first visit to the big city. They were accosted by a beggar. Mr Talbot said he was against giving the man any assistance and had begun to berate him for his idleness. Some beggars, he believed, were quite well-off, plus the man seemed as strong as a horse. But Father gave the man a two-shilling note, saying, 'I can't second guess the man, Tally. Maybe he's hungry. This is not like being in the country where he can pick up mangoes, or eat sugar cane or star-apples or June plums. Look around you, man – just concrete – no trees, no grass, no wild nothing.'

'That was how Sun-Sun was,' Mr Talbot finished. 'Always giving. He gave until it did him in. He gave until he made the supreme sacrifice. That is why we're here today. To remember and to honour the man who was a giver to the end – Sun-Sun Johnson.'

Mrs Benton, whom we fondly called Baba, bent with age and perhaps a touch of osteoporosis, too, was next on the podium. She wore a small hat perched atop her steel-grey hair. A hurricane had all but destroyed her humble abode, she said, but Sun-Sun had fixed it 'good', fixed it better than it was before, fixed it with lumber and zinc that he bought in Sav-la-mar. At no cost to her, she said. He was a good man.

But Father was not always a good Samaritan, as Frank Billet let us know. He and my Father had gone to a village some two miles away to a dance. That, of course, was during their salad days. But they soon found out they weren't welcome. It seemed some fellows from our small town had made some trouble at a previous dance. Frank and my father were told to leave or face some unpleasant consequences.

Well, two against a host of hostile men didn't offer good odds, so they left, or so the village men thought. Father had his brand of payback. He knew the area well and knew where some cowitch grew by the roadside. Now cowitch is a vine-like plant, bearing pods like beans, but larger. The pods are covered with fine hairs, harmless when they are green but deadly when dry. In a strong wind the dry hairs are blown about and can set off some unpleasant scratching by anyone unlucky enough to pick up a few on their skin.

Using his flashlight, Father had carefully scraped some of their fine itchy hairs into his handkerchief. Then with his penknife he cut a small bamboo stem and removed the two joints so that he was left with a hollow pipe. Into this he carefully poured the itchy hairs to make a deadly blowgun.

Already the congregation were trying to stifle their laughter. Anyway, Frank said, they returned to the dance hall, found a chink in a wall and pumped the cowitch into the building. Then they returned to their bicycles, ready to flee the scene. It wasn't long before the revellers began to tumble from the hall, scratching like mad, some men even seeking out the wall and wriggling against it to get at their backs, unreachable by hand. The two pedalled fast out of there, gratified that they had scored one for the home team.

The congregation erupted in unrestrained laughter.

Then it was my turn to eulogize my father. I was only seventeen, but I felt like twenty or older. Only a boy, but I had the courage of a man.

My first memory of my father, I began, was as a tot when he came home from Green Island on banana day. I remembered him coming in with one or two coils of rope slung over his shoulders. The ropes were for the cows and mules, to 'tie them out' so they couldn't get into the fields and destroy them. But ropes were of little interest to me. It was the sweet enchanting aroma of peppermint that followed him into the room. He always brought that, and he'd break off a piece and hand it to me and I was the happiest child in the entire world. It was always on Monday nights, I later learned, because Mondays were 'banana days', and at that time the fruit was taken by truck and carts to Green Island, a seacoast town. It wasn't a real port, the ship was anchored about a half a mile out in the harbour and the bananas were ferried to the ship in large canoes called lighters.

I ended by saying that my father was a little of everything the previous speakers had said of him. Sometimes a prankster, always a giver. Sometimes a clown and fool but always a good Samaritan. A man's man. But what stood out steadfast as a rock in my memory was that he was a rounded human being: a good father and husband.

I could see Ma squirm in her seat, but it had to be said.

'Some of you may not remember him the way I do. Some of you will say that all he ever was was a buffoon and a fool, but Shakespeare, through the mouth of Mark Antony, said it best: "The evil that men do lives after them, The good is oft interred with their bones." But I say to you: he was everything I want to be, except that if I rise, and I shall, I intend to stay up. I intend to climb from River Bottom up the hill to where we are now. Where the sun first greets our growing town. Where most of you live. Where my father once lived. I shall and I will. Thank you.'

There shouldn't have been any applause, but there was.

Then the crowd mingled, viewing the photographs. It was a good memorial service.

5

Yam hills, curry goat and folk songs

If the memorial service did nothing else, it inspired some men with a spirit of cooperation and brotherly love. After the service, I was mobbed outside the church by several of them rattling off a stream of promises.

'Rami, I hear you plantin' yams an' bananas an' I hear you plannin' a day-fo'-day. Count me in.'

'Me too, Rami.'

'Your father was a good man, Rami. I like the way you talk 'bout 'im. I'll be there. Sat'day, you guys?'

'Right on. Sat'day. We'll be there, Rami. An' you won't owe us nothin'. Your father helped many when he was alive.'

When a group of men came to work without pay for one man, that man owed each of them a day of equal work in return, and this was known in our parts as a day-for-day. But these men were giving of their time for my father's sake, and I would owe them nothing. Nothing but food and drinks.

Saturday, of course, was the best day. These men didn't go to work on Saturdays. Most of the women would be off to market and, instead of playing dominoes or visiting the rum bars, the men had decided to help me out.

The attendees at the service had begun to drift home. Ma was speaking to the Reverend and Mrs Ledbetter. Arlene, Brad and I were waiting for her. Both of them engaged me in a quiz.

ARLENE: Rami, do you like pets?
ME: As well as anyone.
BRAD: What pet do you like best?
ME: Oh, I guess a horse.
ARLENE: A horse! A horse is not a pet. It's too big. A cat can be a pet, and a dog can be a pet, but not a horse.
BRAD: A bird can be a pet.
ME: What is this about pets?
ARLENE: Oh, just a survey we're doing. Aren't we, Brad?
BRAD: Yeah, yeah. A survey. A cat then, big brother?
ME: Good heavens, no. Not a cat. Although they are good mousers, they just hang around the house sleeping most of the time.

(*Brad's eyes were beaming.*)

BRAD: How about a dog, then? They don't sleep that much, and they will follow you around. They make good company and can watch over you.
ME: A dog, much better. Much better.

Actually I missed Max. Had he not been killed he would have been quite big now.

Ma joined us. 'Rami,' she said, 'I'd like you to come home with us. I've got a surprise for you.'

'What a surprise!' Arlene said, giggling. 'Oh la-la.'

'You two haven't been telling tales, have you?' Ma asked.

'No, Ma'am,' Brad replied. 'Would we, Arlene?'

'No, no. Never, never. If we told, it wouldn't be a surprise, would it?'

I was stumped. Try as I might I couldn't figure out what the surprise could be, so I had to endure the suspense until we walked through the gate and I heard the first yap of a dog followed by a cacophony of welcoming barks.

'You bought a dog?' I asked Ma.

'It's for you, silly,' Brad said.

'Surprise!' shouted Arlene.

'Yes, Rami. It's for you. I got him yesterday in Sav-la-mar.'

By now we had reached the backyard where the puppy, a black and white beauty, was straining at its tether, anxious to fawn on one or all of us.

'I don't like the idea of your being alone down that rotten place you call home. Max was killed. This is a replacement. The pup is only six months old, but it will be company and in time a watch dog.'

'Thanks, Ma.' I kissed her on the cheek. 'Do you really think I'm in danger, Ma?'

'I don't know. But Jake's not a nice man. He seems capable of bad things. He went after your father to destroy him and did so, and there's no telling that he won't come after you, too. His arch-enemy is dead and gone, but you have replaced him. I don't want anything happening to you.'

'I'll be all right, Ma.'

'Yes, maybe. Until you begin to succeed. If you succeed.'

'Not *if*, Ma, but *when*.'

'What are you going to name the puppy, Rami?' Brad asked.

'Call him Crayfish,' suggested Arlene.

'What kind of stupid name is that?' Brad upbraided her. 'Girls! I think Gunsmoke is a whole lot better. Call him Gunsmoke, Rami.'

'I'll think on it, Brad. And when I see you again, I'll have a name appropriate for the little fellow.'

'Gunsmoke?' Arlene showed her disdain by puckering her face. 'Such a stupid name.'

'It's better than Crayfish,' Brad pointed out.

The sun still shone up here in town, but down where I lived the shadows were spreading like ink through blotting paper.

I took my new companion home. Ma was right. I needed a dog. It would act like an alarm system if any unsavoury character trespassed on my property. I didn't know what I'd do if it happened, but it would be enough that I would be awake and ready.

Jake was indeed in an unpredictable mood. He had cocooned himself in his lodgings at his store and was drinking heavily. He seemed to be planning something, but what?

There would be no point in striking at me now. I had nothing to lose. A better time would present itself if he thought I was succeeding, if and when my promised climb from River Bottom up to the summit started to become a reality.

I took the pup into the house and set out a dish of milk for him and gave him some chicken bones, relics of that day's dinner. He wasted no time exercising his puppy teeth on the bones.

I found my name for the pup. I didn't much fancy Gunsmoke as his name, but it suggested a kindred name – Bullet. Bullet it would be.

Saturday rolled around and Alfred arrived at the crack of dawn. He was good at doing many things, and butchering a goat was one of them. He would take care of the young he-goat which we were going to cook to feed the men who were volunteering their time and muscles. I was no good at killing things so I went up to get Arlene and Brad. I was committed to feeding them tidbits of life close to the earth, and this was such an opportunity.

Those townswomen who were going to market were moving off, some going east to the Grange Hill market, while others were heading west to the market at Green Island. Each market offered something different, for instance the Green Island market was always well stocked with fresh fish brought in by the fishermen of Negril, and Grange Hill was well stocked with beef and pork, and clothing.

The mule-drawn carts crunched along the gravel-covered road, laden with ground produce. The drivers cracked their whips near the haunches of the mules, all the while blowing whistles, their version of the vehicular horn.

If the women had any produce in the carts, they generally walked behind them, balancing on their heads 'pudding pans' made of tin. Why they were called pudding pans was a mystery to me because they were only used for carrying produce on the outward journey, and fish and slabs of beef bought in the market on the return trip.

My sister and brother were looking forward immensely to spending the day at River Bottom and were delighted by the welcome they received from Bullet when we got back.

Brad patted the pup. 'Well,' he said, straightening up. 'So, what did you name him?'

I told him.

'Ah. What's wrong with Gunsmoke?'

'Can't you see, Brad?' I soothed him. 'Gun, Gunsmoke, Bullet. Your name suggested Bullet to me. Don't you think it's a good name?'

'A swell name,' agreed Arlene, happy to learn that Brad's name had been rejected because he had made fun of Crayfish when she had suggested it.

'I guess it's all right,' Brad conceded.

It was time for breakfast, the first for Alfred and me, and the second one for my sibs. While he butchered the goat, Alfred had tended the pot of cooking bananas, and the fruit was now ready. I fixed the trimmings to go with the boiled bananas: fried goat kidney and liver.

While I fried the meat, Brad and Arlene wandered around, looking with interest at the two sides of goat hanging from a low branch of the mango tree, and the skin of the goat tacked to the trunk to cure.

Bullet sniffed where the spilled blood had reddened the grass, but it had all been sopped up by the thirsty soil and what had remained had been licked up by the young sun.

The four of us were just finishing breakfast when the first of the men arrived, their hoes slung across their shoulders.

Bullet yapped at each arriving worker – a good sign, a watchdog in the making. I patted his head. 'Good dog, Bullet.'

By ten o'clock the workforce was in full swing, chopping the earth open with swift, powerful downswings of their hoes, mincing the clods with smaller chops and forming hillocks of the chewed-up soil. As the men broke open the rich soil, exposed fat worms hurried to slide back into it before they were eaten for lunch. My free-run hens and rooster had a feast gobbling up the slow ones.

The sun had scaled the hills and was heating not only the land but the toiling bodies so that, one by one, the men discarded their shirts to be cooler. It was fascinating for us to watch the sweating, rippling muscles glinting in the sun and to hear the men's folk songs.

The common themes of the songs were, of course, work, money and relationships – like this one, which describes women carrying heavy loads to market.

> Ooman a heavy load
> Ooman a heavy load
> Ooman a heavy load
> When Saturday morning come.
>
> When de money nuh nuff (repeated three times)
> Dem call yuh maama man
> Dem call yuh hooligan
> Dem call yuh wukless man.
>
> When de money nuff (repeated three times)
> Dem call yuh honeybunch
> Dem call yuh sweetie-pie
> Dem call yuh sugarplum.

Brad and Arlene were torn between admiring the bodies in motion and the cooking that was now under full steam. Two washed-out kerosene-oil tins, one holding yams, the other rice, were bubbling away on the fire, alongside a cast-iron pot containing curry goat. Brad and Arlene squatted by the fire, stoking it with firewood and getting smoke in their eyes and thoroughly enjoying themselves. Come Monday, they would boast to their classmates of the big cook-out in which they had played a major part.

But soon I put them to work. I made them take lemonade and distribute it to the sweating men. They were very happy to help, and when they asked for more tasks, I told them to rinse the plates we would be eating from.

Alfred and I were the chefs. Of course we didn't cook all the meat. A hind quarter was left in reserve for Ma's larder, and Alfred laid claim to the goat head and about four pounds of meat. Singed and scraped of all hairs, the goat head would be chopped up and made into a soup which in the local lingo went by the name of 'mannish water'. Every man swore by 'mannish water' as a tonic and aphrodisiac.

Everything was going well. The fire crackled, the stokers stoked, and the air was fragrant with the aroma of curry goat. Meanwhile the valley still reverberated with folk songs, including this one:

> Carry me ackee go a Linstead market,
> Not a quatty wut sell.
> Carry me ackee go a Linstead market
> Not a quatty wut sell.
>
> Oh Lawd! Not a mite not a bite,
> Wat a Satiday night!
> Lawd! Not a mite not a bite,
> How de pickney fe feed?

The men were in a race to see who would finish his row first: ten of them, rippling muscles glinting in the strengthening sun, ten rows of yam hills, marching up the hillside.

Then the food was steaming ready. The men rested their hoes and came down from the hill. They washed their hands in the river, then dug in. The curry goat not only gave off an inviting aroma but it yellowed the rice and chunks of yams that the men heaped onto their plates. They ate heartily, and so they should, to replenish all that carbohydrate and protein they had expended.

Brad and Arlene could scarcely contain their delight – eating this feast on the grass! Bullet had a rollicking good time catching bits of curried meat thrown to him and snatching bones to chew on with his puppy teeth.

From time to time we cooled off the hot lunch with gulps from the large jugs of lemonade.

After lunch the men relaxed on the grass, some of them mincing tobacco and filling their pipes for a smoke.

One turned to Arlene. 'Well, Miss, you enjoyin' you'self? How you like this rough lunch?'

'I like it fine,' she answered.

'Diff'rent from 'ome cooked, wouldn't you say?'

She nodded.

Brad got his twopence in: 'And we didn't have to sit up straight, and no table to keep our elbows off. I like the change.'

'I can see you's a upcomin' bushman,' said another.

'There's a little o' Sun-Sun in all o' you,' commented one.

'All right, all right,' decided the one called Dudley. 'Time to go back to work and finish the job.'

So to the hill they returned while Alfred and I washed up.

6

Donna Rae

Since the memorial service I hadn't seen much of Donna Rae. It seemed she was taking pains to keep her distance, but one day I ran into her.

'Hi, Donna,' I said. 'Where have you been hiding?'

'Nowhere. Why?' She seemed uncomfortable.

'Because I haven't seen you around.'

'You know how it is . . . not knowing what to say.' Her eyes went to her feet.

Many people don't know how to deal with tragedy. They want to console but are afraid to say the wrong thing and, perhaps, to reopen healing wounds.

'Yes, yes,' I told her, 'I understand. Don't worry about it.'

Donna Rae looked fine, splendid in fact. We were of the same age, but you know how it is with girls. They develop faster than boys when they reach puberty. She was beautiful.

Her mother was a single parent. Donna's father had died when she was still young. Mrs Hilcher was ambitious and worked hard at various enterprises to provide for her daughter and herself. When she wasn't catering for weddings, she was baking and selling to those people who loved their loaves home-made. Whenever there was a dance or garden party or even a cricket match, Mrs Hilcher would be there with a concession stall of baked goods, beef patties and ginger beer. She was also a very good seamstress, sewing for many women, including brides and their maids. An enterprising woman.

They weren't wealthy, but they were certainly not dirt-poor, either.

They used to live across the river from us, Father and I, but they had moved to a better house near the square, Jake's former house. It was better for both mother and daughter because living down where I was was certainly not conducive to social development. An environment was generally either a plus or a minus, and River Bottom had many negatives.

I was sorry to see them go, but that was progress. In time I too hoped to move up from down there. I missed seeing Donna Rae more often, missed too the flicker of their lights at night through the trees – little mercies that went far in the way of company.

With every passing minute Donna Rae was becoming more at ease.

'What's this I hear, Rami, that you've quit school?'

'There's some truth in that rumour, Donna Rae, but I'm not quitting my education. I'll be doing the GCE – self-taught but with some help from Ma, Mr Dumfries and Mrs Quill. But you heard what I said at the memorial service – I want to avenge my father, redeem his name and succeed where he failed.'

'Rami,' she said, with a gleam in her eyes, 'it's noble of you to take up your father's fight, but can you do both – that and completing your education, too?' After a pause she asked: 'What subjects are you planning to take?'

'Planning? I've already begun: O Level English, and Geography, History and British Constitution at Advanced Level.'

'Maybe we can do some English exercises together,' she said. 'I'm doing O Level English, as well.'

'Of course, Donna Rae,' I said. 'That would be swell.'

She noticed Bullet, who was sniffing shrubs by the side of the road. 'Your dog?'

'Uh-huh. Like him?'

'He's cute. Didn't know you had a new dog.'

'Oh, he's hot out of the litter – a gift from Ma to me, for protection. I've taken to the little fellow quite a bit. Come, Bullet.'

'Bullet?' she commented. 'Cute name.'

'Not bad,' I said.

With lingering looks we parted. I enjoyed our little talk and was looking forward to our studying English together.

A few days later she and I met for our first study session, at River Bottom. We began by doing some exercises in paraphrasing. We selected the same passage, then timed ourselves to complete it in half hour. I checked hers and she mine, then we compared results. Next we did a précis of a twelve-hundred word passage, with the aim of reducing it to two-thirds of its length. Again she checked mine and I hers. We teased each other about our mistakes and discussed improvements. It was fun to be working together. Then it was on to Jane Austen's *Northanger Abbey*.

'How many chapters of the book have you read?' I asked.

'I've just finished chapter thirteen.'

'What d'you think of the characters so far?'

'The Morlands – Catherine and her brother, James – seem likeable enough, but I can't say the same for the two Thorpes, Isabella and her brother, John. The brother seems a real rake.'

'How so?' I pumped her. 'Why a rake?'

'You know as well as I do. Haven't you read as far as I?'

'Of course I have. Just checking on your character analysis. I agree with you. John Thorpe thinks a whole world of himself. He even lies to get his way. He's overbearing and as false as a six-shilling note.'

'As the English would say, he's a rotter,' Donna Rae added.

'OK,' I said, 'so much for John Thorpe. What of Isabella?'

Donna Rae contemplated the question, then she said: 'There's something false about her, too. She gushes too much. Like a porter brimming with too much froth. She seems fake to me.'

'Wow!' I said. 'Nicely put. I agree with you. So, do you think that Catherine and Henry Tilney will eventually tie the knot?'

'It's possible. I like them both. And I think they both like each other enough to make a compatible couple. But we'll have to read on to find that out, won't we?'

'Right. Then let's set a goal. Let's say that by next study session we read up to chapter twenty.'

'At least,' she said.

'Settled.'

'And remember we have Pope to do as well.'

'Don't remind me,' I sighed. 'So much to read.'

Putting the books and paper away we began to chit-chat.

'What did you have for dinner?' I asked, a bit nervous that we were not involved with academic things.

'Rice-and-peas overlaid with slices of roast beef and gravy.' Knowing that I wasn't a good cook, she was hoping to to make me drool.

'And you?' she asked.

If she thought she had crippled me, she was wrong.

'Oh, I ate at Ma's. Cucumber and tomato salad – that was the first course – followed by lobster in a curry sauce and served with rice. And a dessert of sliced pineapple.'

'You're boasting,' she said. 'And what did you have last evening?'

'Escoveitched fish with bammy.'

'Liar,' she said, laughing. 'Liar, liar, liar. You don't know how to escoveitch fish, Rami. Stop your lies.'

'OK, I didn't do it myself, not this time,' I admitted. 'Alfred's wife did it. But I fried the bammy to go with it, soaked it in milk and fried it. You know there's nothing very mysterious about doing escoveitched fish. You fry the fish and next . . . and . . . I confess the next stage is a bit fuzzy.'

'OK, you slice onions and a Scotch-bonnet pepper, include some allspice, wholegrain black pepper and vinegar. Bring the lot to a boil, then pour the concoction over the fish and let it soak. That's your first cooking lesson. From me to you.'

'Thank you so much, Donna Rae. I hope there'll be many more. Hundreds even.'

We were looking into each other's eyes, the windows to the soul. I leaned forward, held her hands in mine and kissed her. Our first kiss. It was like a warm coat on a cool evening.

'Rami?' she whispered. Framed like a question it was really a statement.

For me the warm coat feeling gave way to fire that shot down my spine. Zip, zip, wow!

I walked her home in the dusk, which was enveloping the land like a dark cloak. The crickets were fluting and a lone screech owl gapped the enormous space between the hills. The bats were out, zipping this way and that, making temporary grid work against the piece of pale moon that hung in the sky. Me? Holding Donna Rae's hand, I was walking on air.

On her verandah an anxious Mrs Hilcher was awaiting her daughter.

'Ah, there you are,' she said.

'Good evening, Mrs Hilcher,' I said in my most cheerful voice. 'Thanks for the goodies.' She had sent a bag of gizadas with Donna Rae.

'You're welcome, young Johnson,' she acknowledged. 'That was a long study you two put in.'

'Yes'm,' Donna Rae agreed.

By the way she looked from her daughter to me, she knew something special had happened between us. A mother always knows.

I said my goodnights, and Bullet and I went home. I walked all the way back on air – my first kiss. How about that?

7

Jake Hibbertson

One Friday I ran into Jake Hibbertson. He was walking towards me, and not too steadily. Jake walking? He drove around in his Jaguar, everywhere he went, however short the hop. He seemed quite affable, however. 'Hello, young man,' he said.

'Hello, Mr Hibbertson.'

'And what brings you from River Bottom?'

His eyes were deep and hollow and red, with circles under them. Too much drinking I supposed.

'A bit of shopping, Mr Hibbertson.'

'Don't forget to buy from my store, now. I've got everything you'll need.' He paused. He seemed to be thinking of River Bottom and its poor status. 'I don't suppose you'll be needing any sophisticated stuff that my store doesn't have.'

'That's to be seen, Mr Hibbertson. I'll buy from the store of my choice.'

'You . . . !' He stifled a curse. A scowl flickered across his face, followed by the ghost of a smile. 'Very well then, young man. By the way, I've heard you're going to plant yams.'

'You've heard right, Mr Hibbertson. Acres of them.'

'You think you can succeed where Merton failed?'

'My father failed because he made mistakes, sir. Trusted people who shouldn't be trusted. I will be careful with my trust, Mr Hibbertson. Are you worried that I will rise as my father once did?'

'Worried? You're just a boy. Why should I worry?'

'Not just a boy, Mr Hibbertson. A man in a boy's body.'

I could see he was fighting back a growing anger. A boy needling him in this way! But I wanted him to worry.

'Good day, Mr Hibbertson.'

That rankled him. I had upstaged him. He should have dismissed me, not me him. I clearly heard him say under his breath: 'Darn the little whippersnapper.'

I turned to go on my merry way, whistling: 'There's a Brown Girl in the Ring, Tra-la-la-la-la'. As Jake limped away I called after him, 'You're limping, Mr Hibbertson. Hurt your leg?'

'Ah, you noticed. Small accident.'

'Shouldn't you be driving and giving the leg a rest, sir?'

'Young man, don't you know that exercise is good for both body and soul?'

The rumour was he had gone to see an obeah man in Westmoreland, and on his way back he had been involved in an accident with his Jaguar, which was probable being repaired.

Consulting an obeah man was a new low for Jake. The question was why? What was he up to? Surely he didn't think an obeah man's potions could restore health to his ailing business or stop his drinking? That was up to him. So what was on his mind?

People went to an obeah man for different reasons, the most common being to harm a rival. But there were others such as winning someone's love, or having won it keeping it. In such cases the obeah man or woman would provide his or her client with advice or, worse, a potion. So if Jake meant to hurt someone, who then? Most likely Ma. Was he thinking he could win her back? And if it was me he wanted to hurt, did he think he could stop me from succeeding in my venture?

Contrary to popular belief, mostly among the uneducated, obeah dispensers were not adept in necromancy. But they could be dangerous. They were capable of dispensing poisons. Armed with such poisons, a client could secretly lace a rival's food or drink. There was a case of a man who was disputing the paternity of a baby, the mother of whom had alleged was his. Although he claimed he was not the father, he visited the baby often. The baby was always ill, wasting away, so to speak. The mother had learned that the alleged father had visited an obeah person and, being a superstitious woman, was convinced that the obeah dispenser had enlisted a ghost to do the baby in. An autopsy revealed that the infant had not died from any mystic hanky-panky but from arsenic poisoning. The poison was administered by the father, who had obtained it on the advice of the obeah person. Day by day he put a little in the baby's food. He was arrested for murder.

So if Jake's quarry was Ma, she would have to be careful. But how would he get to her? Something slipped into her shoes? Into her food or drinking water? Onto her lipstick? Ma had to be warned. Maybe she too needed a watchdog.

Our small town was growing. It boasted two haberdasheries, a post office, a butcher's shop, two small grocery shops, two elementary schools and a high school. The high school was further fed by two smaller elementary schools in neighbouring villages. We had three churches – an Anglican, a Baptist and a Church of God. A doctor came by once a week to the clinic. The latest addition was a credit union office. What next? A bank? New houses were springing up. More people were moving in.

The town square was flush with people. Friday was pay day for many, and money was flying from pockets to cash tills. Women were spending their earnings, as well as the 'house money' their husbands had given them. Those men who worked the fields during the week were now wearing clean clothes and were ready to celebrate the end of another working week. Alfred was here, also wearing street clothes, but wearing his trademark rubber boots, too. He was married to those boots.

A caravan of donkeys blew into town, on their way to Green Island market from their home in distant St Elizabeth. Their donkey hampers were full of high-quality thyme and scallion, carrots and rope tobacco. Men and women mobbed them. The women were interested in the spices, herbs and vegetables, the men in rope tobacco. Rope tobacco? Tobacco leaves tightly woven into a rope, and cut into shreds and wadded into pipe bowls and smoked. Alfred purchased a yard.

As I went by I took a look in Jake's store. Three men were in the rum bar, but only a spattering of women in the haberdashery and grocery section. There were empty spaces on some shelves where goods sold had not been replaced. What was eating the man? Why had he stopped being the aggressive businessman he used to be? I could make two guesses: the death of his favourite rival and the loss of his trophy wife. My father was no longer alive for him to taunt with his success, and my mother had left him. Perhaps the latter was the unkindest cut of all. Had she remained with him, he could still crow that he had taken both Robin Hill and his wife from my father. But now he had neither. Robin Hill had burnt to the ground. Only the smoke-blackened walls remained: a cruel reminder that one man had given his life to save another who had ruined him.

Kim Sum's rum bar was full of men slamming dominoes down on a table while they slaked their thirst with cold beer. Kim Sum was a Chinese immigrant from Hong Kong. It was to his store that I went. He was all smiles, a short man with a row of gold teeth in his upper jaw and a goatee blackening his chin.

'Hi, Rani,' he greeted me. Whether from habit, or because he found it difficult to pronounce the 'm' in my name, I can't say, but he always called me Rani.

'Hi, Mr Sum.'

'Long time no see, Rani. Where you bin?'

'Here and there, Mr Sum. How are you keeping?'

'Goot, goot. I don't see you comin' from school no more.'

'I quit. I mean I'm taking time off.'

'Not so goot, Rani. School's goot.'

'I'll be back.' To steer the conversation away from myself, I asked, 'Have you any flour?'

'Always got flour. How much you need?'

'Two pounds will do. And a pound of codfish and two pounds of sugar.'

'Hey, slow down, Rani. Take it easy.' Quietly he repeated the order to himself and proceeded to get the items. But soon he came back to school matters. 'My daughter, Lily, you know her? She doing fine in school. You should be in school, too, Rani.'

'I'll be back, Mr Sum.'

'I hope you right, Rani. You's a good boy.'

Lily was in a grade below mine when I attended, and sometimes we walked together returning from school. Sometimes, too, the other boys and I popped into Mr Sum's store to purchase a fritter Mrs Sum made which she called *achee*. Maybe it was Chinese for fritter, and although it was oily we liked it.

Lily was at the other end of the store helping her mother with a bolt of cloth.

'Hi, Lily,' I said and waved.

I was happy to get away from Mr Sum's probing. But he was right. I should be in school.

8

Christmas

Christmas was fast approaching and with it, as with every year as far back as I could remember, came the environmental features that accompanied it.

Wild flowers we had not seen all year burst into bloom. The sugar-cane fields were also a part of the Christmas dress-up. They flowered, shooting a triangular plume of silken tassels atop each shaft, aptly called the cane arrow because of its resemblance to that fabled weapon. Even the air was different – brisker and fresher than usual and brought by a guest wind down from Canada's frozen north, but having shed some of its coldness as it sped through the USA and cloaked itself with some tropic warmth as it skimmed the Caribbean Sea.

Some of the houses were getting fresh coats of paint, fences were being spruced up. Hedges were having their growth trimmed into brush-cuts and lawns were being dressed. If there were trees in the yard, their lower trunks were being whitewashed with limestone, which made them look like giant legs wearing anklets.

Roosters that strutted around their yards like fops and dandies and crowed boastful cock-a-doodle-dos had better watch themselves, because come Christmas morning, many of them would be losing their heads and colourful feathers to fill families' Christmas pots and to stuff pillows, respectively.

This was a bad time for dogs. Firecrackers were an integral part of the Christmas celebrations. I could hear a few of them popping here and there, set off by early revellers. Bullet, who was always eager to accompany me to town to the point of running ahead of me, was now reluctant to go up there. Poor Bullet. And worse was yet to come.

I sold one of my heifers to Mr DeRoche from a neighbouring village. The sale put ten pounds in my hand, part of which would go towards my Christmas shopping, and part towards purchasing yam heads for my yam hills that were waiting to be planted.

To purchase my Christmas presents I took the bus to Sav-la-mar. I bypassed Grange Hill, a town which was closer, because I was hoping that Sav-la-mar being a larger town would have a better selection of presents. I could have gone with Ma, but then she would be privy to my purchases, and I wasn't going to have that.

For Alfred I bought a pair of rugged leather boots which I hoped would protect his feet in the coming year. Yet I feared he would put them away as 'dress boots' and go on trudging to the fields in his trademark rubber boots, which had begun to develop holes.

I had seen Ma too often cradling books in her arms, just like we students did. It was time she had a business-like leather satchel. I bought one for her.

Arlene would get a silver bangle, and at twelve years plus she wasn't too old to have a doll, even if as an ornament, and there was a perfect one staring at me through a store window. I bagged it for her, too.

At his age, ten going on eleven, Brad would coo over a small battery-powered train set.

I didn't forget Donna Rae. That girl was growing on me. For her I found a beautiful umbrella, not too gaudy but colourful enough.

There was Fantasia, too, who brought me dinners cooked with finesse and who tidied the house for me when I neglected to clean it up. How could I leave her off my list? Countless times I had heard her speak of how much people charged to 'straighten' hair, so I bought her a straightening comb. She could learn to heat it on hot coals and hot-comb her hair herself. If some men were capable of trimming their own hair, so could she, with the help of mirrors, 'straighten' her hair herself and save some money. Merry Christmas, Fantasia!

If Friday night is the highlight of the week, Christmas Eve is the party night.

The shops were decorated with ribbons, and streamers hung diagonally and along the walls. The ceilings dripped with balloons of every colour and shape. The shops stayed open for as long as people were in the square.

The night reverberated with the timbre of laughter and chatter, chatter, chatter, and the sporadic bursts of firecrackers followed by 'Chrismus! Chrismus! Hip! Hip! Hooray!' Dogs did not share in this celebration. The poor things were probably cowering under beds or in backyards, and whimpering, too, Bullet included.

There were youngsters everywhere, some as old as I and some younger. The young ones hung on to balloons while they licked lollipops or ate jackass corn, a formidable brittle cake.

The older teenage males, some of whom were hell-bent on impressing girls, were strutting about in a way that would make them noticeable. I saw one – I knew him – Ashton Berbie, riffling through a wad of two-shilling notes with the fingers of one hand. I guessed he had exchanged a pound note for these two-shilling ones to impress on the girls that here was a well-heeled Ashton Berbie. Ashton was short, but with his flamboyance you wouldn't notice it. He wore wedge-heeled shoes, and his long sleeves were always rolled up neatly, almost to his armpits.

But hadn't I slipped up in not taking my sibs along to enjoy this smorgasbord of swirling humanity? I rushed over to Ma's and got them, and they gratefully joined the crowd.

'So many people!' Arlene wondered.

'When do they go to bed?' asked Brad.

'When the stores close, Brad. If and when they do. And even then some will go visiting and stay up all night.'

'Wow! So many balloons! The shops are full of them,' he commented.

'That's Christmas for you.'

I bought them a pack of balloons, some firecrackers and bottles of cream soda. Brad, enjoying his night out, doused his perpetual smile only long enough to sip his cream soda and blow up balloons.

'Can we pop some firecrackers?' he asked.

'Not in this crowd, stupid,' Arlene answered.

'Who's stupid?' he shot back. 'Other people are popping them!' He was right. The air was pungent with the stench of spent explosives.

'So?' Arlene said. 'You're not other people. And not everybody likes to have them pop around them. They frighten people.'

'Some people. Some people like you. Scaredy-cat people.'

'In the morning, Brad,' I promised. 'We'll pop some in the backyard.'

And here came Alfred with his wife. He was wearing a white jipijapa hat and shoes, not rubber boots. Wonder of wonders. His wife wore a colourful head-tie wound up high, African style, matched by a print dress. She was the curtseying type and curtsied to my sibs and I. Arlene curtsied right back to her and Alfred laughed.

I hadn't thought of Alfred as the love-her-tender type, but, seeing him with his arm daintily wrapped around his wife's waist, that thinking went straight out of my head. They moved on and so did we.

Five minutes later we ran into Fantasia and her boyfriend, Dillon Trelawney, a fellow obviously proud to be squiring her, going by the sheer, unchanging flash of his iceberg-white teeth.

'So you brought your sister and brother out to Christmas Eve on the town, Rami.'

'So I did, Fantasia. So I did.'

'Enjoy,' said Dillon Trelawney, as they disappeared into the crowd.

We had to fight our way into Mr Sum's store. Here the decorations had an oriental flavour – pagoda-shaped do-dads and Chinese lanterns by the dozen.

Lily was busy helping customers and passing out free calendars made of fine-slatted bamboo with Chinese characters on them. I squinted at her, and she waved to me and gave me a cat-like smile. I bagged two of the calendars, one for me and the second for Ma.

I was going to spend Christmas with my family so when we left the square, we headed for Ma's house. There wasn't a Christmas tree, but the living room dripped with evidence of the season – stockings and streamers, and wrapped presents in a pile in a corner of the room.

Then it was morning.

Clad in their night clothes my sibs rushed into the living room followed by a drowsy Ma. Fantasia was summoned from kitchen duties.

When Brad saw that Arlene had two gifts from me, and he only had one, he seemed at first crestfallen, even jealous, but when he ripped open the wrapping paper, he realized he hadn't been short-changed. His eyes said it all. They glowed like hot coals and almost popped out of his head.

'For me?' he gasped. 'Wow! Ma, look what I got!' To me he said, 'Does it run?'

'Sure it does. You only have to set up the tracks, pop the batteries in and it'll choo-choo on its merry way.'

'Gee, thanks, Rami,' he said, putting his arm around me.

Arlene thanked me with a kiss on the cheek, and so did Ma. She was ecstatic.

'To think I've wanted to buy myself one of these satchels for the longest time, and now you've beaten me to it. This is really thoughtful, Rami. It will do nicely for my papers and books. Thanks, son.'

Fantasia received her gifts with wide-smile glee – from Ma a pair of pumps, Arlene had a pair of slippers for her, and Brad gave her a hand mirror framed in turtle shell. Together with my comb, her gifts were all about beauty and looking good.

From Arlene I received a box of white handkerchiefs, and from Brad a harmonica.

'Play it when you're lonely,' he advised. 'Especially at night.'

Ma gave me a fountain pen and the newest edition of the *Oxford Dictionary*, an atlas, a History textbook and a book of contour maps. Good old Ma. She was thinking of my studies. They were very appropriate gifts, but there were more: sheets and pillowcases, bath towels and a razor. So she had noticed! Facial hair had begun to peep through.

She was doing her best for me. She was under tremendous pressure. She was being criticized left, right and centre. The talk was excruciating. She had abandoned me to a life of desolation down in the hole, meaning of course River Bottom. She was an unfit mother, etcetera, etcetera.

We enjoyed a hearty breakfast of eggs and bacon, followed by pancakes smothered with syrup. Ma had coffee, and we children settled for cupfuls of hot cocoa with cocoa fat swimming on the surface. Fantasia was a good cook. It was all so very scrumptious.

Hardly had we finished eating and were deep into exchanging pleasantries, when we were interrupted by a knock on the door. I went to answer it.

Once a well-dressed man, Jake was now a mess. His clothes looked as if he had slept in them, if he had slept at all.

Very few things smell as bad as stale liquor on a man, and Jake stank. His eyes were red and tired.

'Merry Christmas, young man.'

'And a merry Christmas to you, too, Mr Hibbertson.'

Brad and Arlene were peeping out on either side of me.

A thin smile cracked Jake's tired face as he reached for the two peepers. 'Merry Christmas to you, young ones,' he said.

They said merry Christmas and retreated out of his reach.

'Who is it, Rami?' Ma asked from the dining room.

'Mr Hibbertson, Ma'am.'

'What does he want?'

'Can't I wish you a merry Christmas, Debbie?'

'Merry Christmas, Jake,' she said from where she sat.

'Isn't that a bit impersonal?' he asked. 'Can't you come to the door? Can't I come in?'

I answered the last question for Ma. 'It's not a good idea, Mr Hibbertson, for you to come in.'

His voice changed. 'And why not? Are you speaking for your mother, boy?'

'Yes, I am, Mr Hibbertson. We're having a quiet family time and we'd rather not have it disturbed.'

'Out of my way, you little . . .'

'On your way, Mr Hibbertson. You've said your merry Christmases. Now be on your way.' I stood my ground, blocking the doorway.

Ma came to the door.

'Jake,' she warned, 'we want no trouble. You had best leave us alone. We want no part of you. Can't you get it into your head?'

'You're still my wife, dang it.'

'In name only,' Ma fired back.

'You'll never get a divorce. Never!'

'We'll see about that. Lord, you smell to high heaven of rum. Stale rum. Goodbye.'

That stung him. I could see the shadow of defeat travel across the landscape of his stubbled face. It seemed he wanted to hit somebody. That was when I shut the door and turned the key in the lock.

'You'll have to be careful of that man, Ma.'

'Don't I know it?'

'You heard of his visit to an obeah man?'

'I heard a rumour,' Ma said.

'It's no rumour, Ma. On his way back he had an accident. He smashed the car and injured his leg. He's not limping now, but he was.' I paused. 'But more importantly, why did he go to see an obeah man?'

'Perhaps to buy some potions which he thinks can stop his slide into perdition.'

'A potion, yes, probably, but more seriously, what if it is a poison to slip into somebody's food or drink?'

'What d'you mean, Rami?' Ma frowned.

'You know he's determined to have you, Ma. Have you as his wife. Father's dead. He's got nothing over him anymore. But he needs you. You were his trophy. Father's wife – ex-wife. It's you dead or alive. Be careful. You can't be too careful. There's no black magic in obeah, but an obeah person can be deadly with poisons and potions.'

'Oh Lord,' Ma said. 'I see what you mean. Oh my Lord.'

'You also need a dog, Ma. A dog can sound an alarm and run intruders off.'

'You're so right, Rami. So right.' Ma was upset. I was sorry I had brought it up. It darn nearly ruined our Christmas. But being Johnsons we bounced back.

Firecrackers were popping all over town. My sibs and I retired to the backyard and lit a few, too.

Fantasia was already making preparations for Christmas dinner. The turkey was dressed and ready for the oven, poor chap. His gobble-gobble days had come to an end.

I popped over to Donna Rae's with my umbrella gift. She had a gift for me, too, an alarm clock – so practical. We chatted for a while and I sampled Mrs Hilcher's Christmas punch. It had been a jolly good Christmas.

9
Cripes Randall

Christmas and New Year were behind us.

I had yam heads of my own, but I had to buy a slew from a Mr Guthrie, who had a surplus. Alfred and I began by planting the variety known as negro yams. With hoes we opened the yam hills about one-third down and inserted the heads with the 'eyes' pointing up as one would a potato, then covered them up. When the planting was done, I had a two-acre field. It was just the start.

The dry season was upon us. It was also crop time, the few months during which the sugar cane was harvested and made into sugar, molasses and rum at the sugar factory. It was hard work for the men and women who cut the canes and bundled them, but for children, particularly boys, crop time put them on the very cusp of a bonanza. As the trucks laboured in low gear up the hills, they ran behind and pulled themselves up on the tailgates for rides, but dismounted before the trucks levelled off and picked up speed. And that was not all. As they dismounted they pulled out lengths of sugar cane for chewing on. Just part of the fun. What blissful times!

The section of road which ran through the square was asphalted, but the rest of it was surfaced with broken stones crushed into the roadbed by a steam roller. With the lack of rain and the many trucks running back and forth to the sugar mill at Frome in Westmoreland, there was a lot of dust. It followed the trucks like tails on animals and it powdered everything on either side of the road.

Yam vines were sprouting olive-green from the yam hills, and Alfred and I were busy preparing poles for them to entwine themselves around and climb. Being the tallest and straightest, bamboo was the favoured pole. With the branches trimmed and the footing sharpened to a point, the poles were ready. On a Saturday morning some of the men who had dug the hills returned and helped to stick the poles into the ground. This time they would be paid for their work. I helped, too.

Each of us carried a pan of water which was used to soften the dry earth as we slammed the point of the bamboo poles time and time again into the earth. Each pole had to go deep enough to make it stand firm, because when the vines had climbed to the top and had leafed, the pole would be carrying a heavy burden.

In a few weeks my yam field was a sea of olive-green leaves and vines. The foliage was so thick you could no longer see the bamboo poles. I hired a couple of women to hoe the field, pulling out weeds, digging around the yam hills and stirring up the soil, thereby aerating the hills. I was looking forward to a generous crop.

One night I was woken up by Bullet barking at something outside one of the windows. When I joined him, I saw three cows dining on some of my young banana plants. A fourth was eating my yams.

Dressing quickly, Bullet and I chased them. They headed straight for the place in the barbed wire fence from where they had come. There was something suspicious about the breach. It seemed that someone had deliberately uprooted some posts so the fence at that point was practically lying on the grass. The cows only had to step through.

It was Jake's fence. His pasture, which held about fifteen cows and some mules, abutted on my property on one side.

With the cows safely back in the pasture, I set the posts back in their holes and heaped earth and stones around them.

Thanks to Bullet, who had alerted me in time, the cows had not done too much damage. About twelve young banana plants had some of their leaves ripped off, but they would survive, and the yams had too many leaves to suffer much damage from the loss of a few.

I had to let Jake know I was on to him. I went to see him.

'My cows? Stop your wild accusations, young man. My cows are always pastured. Unlike you and others of your kind, I have a fenced pasture.'

'And so you have, Mr Hibbertson, but just the same your cows were eating my bananas and yams. I drove them back into your pasture and you know it. Someone had deliberately interfered with the fence so they could get out.'

'Watch your mouth, boy. Beware of your slander.'

'The next time . . .'

'Oh? The next time – what? You'll do what? Planting two acres of yams, you twerp! Growing bananas, rearing cows! Do you think that you can compete against me? Replace your loser father? You think you will be my competitor?'

'I'm not in competition with anyone, Mr Hibbertson', I said as calmly as I could. 'I've charted a course and intend to follow it through to the end. No competition. Just free enterprise at work. And I can see it's working – or why would you be worried?'

'Worried? Me?'

'Yes, you. Stay away from my property or there'll be hell to pay.'

'Is that it?' he blurted.

I didn't really see what I could do if there was a next time. Perhaps I could take them to the Green Island pound, but look at the trouble I would have, roping the cows and leading them four miles to the pound, that is if I wasn't intercepted on the way by Jake or his underlings.

Jake had a parting shot. 'I broke your father and I'll break you, too, boy. Break you without letting my cows do my dirty work for me.'

'My father had a soft underbelly, Mr Hibbertson. I'm not hindered by one.'

But the man was up to no good. He was really hurting from my entrance into the agricultural sweepstakes. I could understand his anxiety. A boy, a mere boy. What if I pulled off what seemed to be the impossible? The town would rise up behind me and against him.

What would he do next? A few nights later, about midnight, I had my answer. Bullet once again was on the job. He was not barking this time, only growling.

When I looked out of the living room window, I saw no one, but the pup soon pointed me in the right direction – towards the rear of the house.

This time it was someone, not cows. A man was sneaking up to the house. The moon was high and the landscape was pale yellow with light. What was the intruder up to? He seemed to be Cripes Randall, one of Jake's lackeys. Was Jake's obeah meant for me and not Ma? And was Cripes sent to deliver whatever it was?

I collected water which ran from the eaves via a gutter into a barrel, water I used for washing dishes and more importantly for cooking. Was he about to spike the water with something toxic? I would have to discourage him.

I had an idea. Left over from my Christmas celebrations were a half a dozen really large firecrackers we referred to as bombs. They could boom like a gun. It was going to scare Bullet, but it had to be done. I got one and quietly went outside in the opposite direction to the intruder. I lit and tossed it.

I leaned around the corner of the house and when the firecracker boomed it had the desired effect. The man jumped a full two feet into the air and yelled, 'Cripes!' Amazingly he had yelled out his own name, because I later confirmed that it was indeed Cripes Randall.

He was limping as he ran.

Cripes was indeed an odd name. His father, Manny Randall, had saddled him with that cussed name. Manny was at least a foot shorter than his wife, but he compensated for the deficit with uncommon stubborness. When it came to having the last word, he wrote the rule. When his son was born, he was so overwhelmed with joy that his first word was 'Cripes!'

His wife should have known not to ask him a foolish question, but she did: 'Is that what you mean to call our son? Cripes?'

Well, Manny had intended to name the boy Emmanuel after himself, but when his wife questioned his reaction, he couldn't resist having the last word.

'Why not?' he asked. 'It's a good name, aint it?'

So the unfortunate baby was christened Cripes Randall, a real travesty. To save himself from the torment of other boys at school, Cripes dropped out of the fourth grade. For a while he worked with his father, then when he was older, he went to work for Jake.

The next day while I was up at the square I ran into Cripes. He was limping. My suspicion was confirmed. He was indeed the culprit who had sneaked into my yard to do whatever evil he was sent to do.

In my most cheerful voice I said: 'Hi, Cripes, what's wrong, man? I see you're limping. Sprained something?'

He knew that I knew. He was avoiding looking at me and he took the tack that the best kind of defence was aggressive offence.

'Wot you come axin' me 'bout limpin' for? It's my business.'

'Take it easy, Cripes. Can't I show an interest in my fellow man? Did you trip over something while you were running, perhaps?'

'Leave me alone.'

'Be careful next time, Cripes. You were lucky this time. It could've been worse. A broken leg, maybe.' Then I delivered my *coup d'état*. 'A gun can do a world of damage.'

Cripes was sweating. He said nothing to my last words. He limped away, and he was more upset than when I ran into him. That suited me fine.

Mondays were banana days, when farmers reaped their mature fruit and took them to the roadside to be graded. I had a few mature bunches, and Alfred and I loaded them into the cart and took them up to the station where the grader would come and grade the fruit and issue vouchers.

The grader travelled in a convertible car, which we locals referred to as a 'cloth top'. He was very good at his job, very glib. As fast as the men lifted the bunches he was calling out the grades.

'Seven hands, six hands, eight hands, eight, six, bunch, seven, seven, bunch, reject – not mature enough – seven, bunch, reject – bruises on the fruit – bunch, eight . . .', and so on. A bunch of bananas had nine hands or more.

As fast as his boss rattled off the grades, his assistant wrote them down, and when it was all over he issued vouchers to each of us. The fruit that passed the test would be trucked to Lucea, a town which had long supplanted Green Island as the banana port.

10

Staying on at River Bottom

Another Friday evening and I was in the square, peopled generously as usual. Joe Canata was revving up the mood with his banjo, plucking away and singing, 'Brown Gal in the Ring'. Joe was sitting on a culvert where the younger crowd had surrounded him and were singing along with him.

Kim Sum's store was doing roaring business. His wife and his daughter, Lily, manned the fabric and fine goods section, while Kim attended to grocery orders, or slipped from time to time into the bar to serve thirsty men beer, rum or soda.

And whom should I run into at the last minute? Donna Rae. She was buying flour, sugar and spices for her mother's baking.

I walked her home, helping her carry the bags. With every passing day she was looking more beautiful. She was one reason I was sorry I quit school. Were I still there, I'd be seeing her more often. Or was it better this way, that we weren't too much in each other's company, thereby making our meetings much more meaningful? What do they say – absence makes the heart grow fonder? Maybe this was the better way. Anyway, she and I had another study date on Sunday afternoon, at her home.

After we had exchanged pleasantries, she got onto what was bothering her. 'You know, Rami, I think you ought to leave River Bottom and move in with your mother.'

'And why is that, beautiful one?'

'Because . . . because for one thing it would be safer. I've heard of your trouble with Mr Hibbertson.'

'No big thing. Nothing I can't handle. And for another thing?' I asked.

'It's just not right for you, at your age, to be living by yourself, cooking your own food. You can't even cook. You'll waste away if you continue to eat poorly.'

'But I do eat properly, Donna Rae. My diet consists of protein, carbohydrate, vegetables and fruit. And when I say fruit I mean mangoes, when they're in season, pineapples, which are always in season, jackfruit, June plums and otahiti apples. I get plenty of fruit. Girl,' I said spinning around, 'don't I look healthy? Actually I'm not alone in the food department. My Ma drops by to check on me, and she often sends Fantasia with dinners for me. To be frank I wish she weren't so attentive. A boy shouldn't be pampered if he is to become a man.'

'You can say anything you want. I'm convinced you ought to live with your family.'

'I'm safe, and I'm eating right. What's the problem?' I asked.

'You and Mr Hibbertson,' she continued. 'You're going to let that man destroy you.'

'Fat chance. I can take care of myself.'

'I don't mean just physical destruction, Rami.'

'Then what?'

'I mean destroying you as a person. If you let this competition with him get the better of you . . .'

'What competition? I'm not in competition with him. I'm just carrying out a promise I made to myself.'

'Hate can destroy a person from within, Rami.'

'I don't hate Jake. At least I don't think I do.'

'You're so stubborn,' she said, stomping a sneaker-clad foot.

'And you . . . you're so beautiful even when you're angry.'
'Will you stop? Stop saying it.'
'The truth will prevail.'
'And this is not all about you. You should think of your mother. People are villifying her, saying that she has abandoned you.'
'Yes, yes. I know about that, but we can't let others set our agendas for us, can we?'

We were passing a large cotton tree which stood guard over the road. A truck went by. Lights were on in the houses. A dog barked somewhere and was answered by several others, including Bullet, who did his puppy yaps.

Donna Rae changed the subject. 'How are your studies coming on?'

'Fine. But the kerosene lamp light is beginning to affect my eyes. Sometimes they burn a lot.'

'Maybe you should start studying earlier when there's still some daylight.'

'It's an idea,' I admitted. 'But you know I like waking up at three and four o'clock in the morning and studying when the body is rested and the brain is wide open and receptive.'

Before we parted I reminded her of our Sunday afternoon study date. I loved that girl. Although she was wrong about my intent to stick it out at River Bottom, I was impressed. What perception in one so young!

'Walk good,' she said as we parted.

A few days later I ran into Cripes Randall. He was sitting on a tree stump near where the road began to dip towards River Bottom. He seemed down in the mouth.

'What's up, Cripes?' I greeted him.

'Not much, Rami.' This was a warmer Cripes than the one with whom I had had a duel but a few days ago. He seemed even anxious to engage me in conversation. And I was ready to oblige.

'Not working today?' I asked. I touched my forehead in a gesture of recall. 'Oh, pardon me. I forgot about your injured leg, Cripes.'

'No mo' work fo' me, Rami. I got fired.'

'You don't say. Why?'

Cripes kept his eyes on the ground. 'I got a confession to make. It was me that come into you yard de odder night. Missa Jake want me to mek trouble fo' you.'

I pumped him. 'What kind of trouble?'

'To set you cows loose so dey could eat you bananas an' yam leaves. Then it would be you own animals eatin' you plants. He even hope they would wander away an' somebody would take 'em to the pound.' He lifted his eyes. 'Sorry, Rami.'

'Apology accepted, Cripes. You were only following orders. But why did he fire you? You did your best, I think.'

'When he see me talkin' to you de odder day, he said I was lettin' the cat out the bag. Tellin' you 'bout the plan. Said I was workin' wit' you behind 'is back.'

'I see. He's a hard man, Cripes.'

'You can say dat again, Rami.'

'Hmm,' I said. I could see an opportunity to capitalize on this development. Alfred was a good man, but he was getting long in the tooth. Here was a muscled young man, strong as a horse and only twenty-two or thereabouts.

'Well, Cripes,' I began, 'if you're looking for work, I could use a good man down at River Bottom.'

He shot to his feet. 'You mean dat, Rami?'

'Sure do, Cripes. You can start tomorrow.'

'You not angry wit' me?'

'Nope,' I said.

Throwing his cap in the air, he jumped with joy, but when he landed, it was with some sorrow. The poor chap had forgotten about his sore ankle. It didn't seem to hurt too much, though. 'I'll be dere tomorrow,' he vowed.

And he was. He was there even before the sun had licked up the mist from River Bottom, and I soon found out why he was so early.

Those bachelors who worked for Jake shared a small building behind the store as their living quarters. Now that Cripes had been sacked, he was homeless. Unless he returned to his parents' home, which for most grown men is not an option, he had no place to live.

I decided to do something that was a long-standing taboo. A property owner did not share his living quarters with field hands, but I would. I had a spare room which was separated from my bedroom by the yawning living-dining room. Cripes would not only be company, he would be useful muscle. Jake would have to think twice about sending another troublemaker while Cripes was with me.

I told Cripes he could have it for a while.

With a gleaming white-teeth smile he thanked me.

As a matter of fact I had thought of moving in with Ma, coming down in the days to work the farm, but Jake's two attempts to do mischief had made me change my mind. Imagine the damage he could inflict at night if the farm were left unguarded. I could imagine why he was so intent on foiling me. I was yet a boy, and if I pulled off the comeback my father had begun, it would be too big a humble pie for him to swallow. But I was full steam ahead. He would have to eat that pie yet.

Cripes wasted no time. After he had had breakfast with me, he went about slashing down the thick, almost jungle-like growth that had never been cleared – space for my expanding banana field.

The next day he turned to another job. We were going to spray the banana field. Panama disease, brought by workers returning from helping to build the Panama Canal, had wiped out the Gros Michel variety of bananas. Its replacement, the lacatan, suffered from its own flaw – leaf spot – a brown spot that appeared on a leaf or leaves, which, if left untreated, would spread until the whole lot were consumed and died. To arrest the spread of the leaf spot, the leaves were periodically sprayed with a mixture of lime and bluestone.

Some of the bigger farmers had motorized pumps, but I had the manual type which was set in motion by a shoulder-high lever rocked back and forth. Cripes was perfect for powering it. Alfred manned the spray gun. My job was to set the second barrel in a new location and fill it with water for the next batch of lime and bluestone mixture.

Cripes's dancing muscles rippled with what seemed like joy as he rocked the lever back and forth non-stop until the pump had sucked the last of the blue solution from the barrel. The work sped by like something pleasant. He was definitely a coup.

Ma had taken up my suggestion and had obtained a pup, apparently from the same litter as Bullet. Brad was ecstatic, and he had graduated from wanting to call the rascal Gunsmoke, the name he had chosen for my pup, and instead he named the new one, Cudjoe.

Cudjoe had been a famous maroon chief in Jamaican history. The maroons were runaway slaves who established themselves on the mountain, descending at nights to raid and wreak havoc on the sugar estates from which they had escaped. Their guerrilla tactics became such a thorn in the side of the British authorities that, to appease them, they were given some form of autonomy.

Ma was pleased with the name Cudjoe. She liked the fact that Brad had begun to associate present-day things with historical data.

Cudjoe for Brad's pup, Bullet for mine, and they were brothers. Whenever I visited Ma, Bullet was sure to accompany me, and the two pups would sniff each other in greeting before running to play in the backyard.

Meanwhile my nest egg at the credit union was increasing pound by sterling pound. I had just banked eight pounds from the sale of bananas, and every banana day I was expecting to take in an equivalent sum – for now, because the amount would increase as my field grew.

I sold a heifer for twelve pounds. Two of my cows were in calf and I had four goats – two breeding shes, a he and two kids. The she-goats would continue to produce kids, which would bring in money. But the big money was in the yam field. From the luxuriant foliage of the yams and knowing the soil was virgin, I expected a big yield when they came on stream later.

11
'No man is an Island'

I decided to have a heart-to-heart talk with Cripes. I told him I'd like him to do some school work. His reaction was a bit hostile.

'Wot for?' he asked.

'Because without schooling you won't get far in this world, Cripes. You've been working for Jake since you were old enough, haven't you?'

'So?' he asked, pouting.

'Digging yam hills, tending his animals, working in his fields, loading and unloading his truck, haven't you?'

'So? I do that fo' you.'

'Yes, but you can do better, Cripes. In time you can become my right-hand man. My main man.'

His eyes took on a glimmer of interest.

'So to become that you'd have to brush up on your schooling. Learn how to read and write properly and do some arithmetic.'

'I don' know, Rami. Arit'me what?'

'You remember what you did in grade four before you quit, Cripes? Adding numbers, subtracting them, multiplying?'

'Wot you want me doin' all dat fo'? You don' go to school no more. So wot you want me to do all dose darn t'ings fo'?'

'But I haven't given up on school, Cripes. Certainly you must see my light on at three and four o'clock some nights.

It's because I'm studying. I teach myself and I get help from my mother and two other teachers at school.'

'You can do dat? Teach you'self?'

'Oh yes, I read the textbooks, I make notes.' I showed him the books. The sheer size of them made him step back.

'Cripes!' he blurted out.

Wonderful, wasn't it? Imagine the singular oddity of being able to verbalize surprise by using your own name!

'So you see,' I persisted, 'I can teach you. If you can brush up on your reading, writing and arithmetic, you may one day be asked to be my headman.'

'Headman?' His eyes were wide open now to the point of bulging. 'Headman,' he mused. 'I'll t'ink 'bout it, Rami. I'll t'ink 'bout it.'

But he didn't have to think a long time. The status of headman was egging him on.

To gauge where he was in writing skills, I asked him to write a description of the tree beside the house.

It was almost funny to see a grown man writing so intently, with the tip of his tongue emerging between his lips – just like a fourth grader might do when concentrating. This is what he wrote:

> *De mangoh tre is big it tallah more dan de hose it got ~~plendly~~ plenty branch an it got lotso leaf it got blasum an lotso bees flyin roun de blasum dem. Wan day it will bare mangohs, mangohs cum out small, small like cashoo nut an dey ~~grin~~ green. Dey grow green til dey get big ~~big~~ den dey ~~tun~~ turn yallah an red like miss taler chik alwes red. heh, Ripe mangohs swit, green mangohs sower. I like mangohs.*

After I had checked the paragraph I told him his description was quite good, but we had a lot of work to do in spelling and punctuation. I saw possibilities in this grown-up fourth grader. I was pleased with his dash of humour about Miss Taylor's cheeks being red. Miss Taylor was an old spinster who rouged her cheeks mercilessly red and reddened her lips to match.

I didn't throw the paragraph out. I meant to use it at a later date.

We started work in earnest on phonics, letter blends – *ph, dr, sp, th*, and so on. Then on to syllabication – how to divide words into syllables, pointing out that each syllable must have a vowel in it.

Cripes's progress was slow, but he was determined. He not only had his sights set on becoming a headman but he was grateful for the way I was treating him as an equal. Nobody so far, nobody besides his parents, had done so. Here he was being given a chance to improve his schooling.

Next we ventured into the world of arithmetic, adding first single-digit numbers then double- and onto triple-digits. It was almost funny to see the man counting on his fingers, just like the grade-four students might even then be doing in schools around the country. His progress sweetened his resolve – so much so that he reminded me that it was 'school time' whenever I was late cracking the whip. Subtraction was a bit more challenging for Cripes. He had a difficult time trading numbers. Whenever the ones or tens were higher in the subtrahend than those in the minuend, he tended to reverse the order and take the smaller number from the bigger:

$$\begin{array}{r} 75 \\ -68 \\ \hline 13 \end{array}$$

So instead of taking the 8 ones from the 5 by trading, he took the easy way out and subtracted five from eight. It took a long time to get him over this hurdle, but he was determined to learn, and what more could one ask?

Ma was furious about our living arrangements.

'What's happening to you, Rami? How can you let this boy move in with you?'

'Man, Ma, not boy.' I was game to a bit of needling.

'Your father, with all his shortcomings, never sank this low. He had his ways, but he also had his pride. Don't you know that a property owner does not share the same roof with the working field hands? The separation of management from labour, Rami.'

'Ma, listen to me. Cripes is more than a labourer. He's like a bodyguard to me. Jake must be taken seriously. As a matter of fact I had thought of moving in with you, then Jake made his moves and I called it off.'

She softened. 'You did? You meant to move in with us?'

'Sure did. I don't like what people are saying about you. That you've abandoned me and all that nonsense. But when Jake sent Cripes to do his mischief, I knew I had to stay down there a while longer. Think what he could do to my fields at night if I weren't there! If we weren't there!'

'So how can you trust that character, Cripes? What if he's a spy working secretly for Jake?'

'No, Ma'am. I may still be a teen, but I am a fairly good judge of character. He's with me all the way. I'm even teaching him to read and write and do arithmetic.'

She softened to the point of smiling. 'Just like your father,' she said. 'In his heyday he picked up all kinds of strays and made men out of them.'

'As they say, Ma, one hand washes the other, or, if you scratch my back, I'll scratch yours.'

'I still don't feel comfortable about it,' she mumbled. 'What will people think? What will they say?'

'You worry too much about what people say, Ma.'

'I have to. I have a position in the community. I'm a teacher for goodness' sake. To have my son living with his labourer!'

I resorted to literature. 'Let me quote from the great poet, John Donne himself: "No man is an Island entire of itself; every man is a piece of the Continent, a part of the main . . . Any man's death diminishes me, because I am involved in Mankind; And therefore never send to know for whom the bell tolls; it tolls for thee".'

'Boy,' she blurted, 'do you think you can sidetrack me with fancy words, do you? I wasn't born yesterday. Stick to the subject.'

But to me that last bit of fuming was fake. In those eyes of hers and in the twitching of her upper lip was a sense of pride in me for quoting that passage as a lever. She was a lover of learning and those who pursue it. That quote won me the argument.

Brad and Arlene were standing by, smiling as they lapped up the battle of words. When they got me aside, Arlene asked: 'Where did you learn such fancy stuff, Rami? I don't understand it, but how I love the sound of those words!'

'I read a lot, Sis, and I stumble on some good stuff.'

'Wow!' said Brad. 'D'you think I could pick up on such words some day?'

'Of course, Bro, in time. Wait a minute, you two. You're not thinking of using quotations on Ma, are you?'

They giggled.

'You bet,' said Brad.

'You make her so angry, Rami. And yet she isn't angry at all,' Arlene commented. 'How d'you do it?'

'It takes tact, my child. Tact and practice.'

Obviously they liked the way I was able to needle Ma lovingly.

We went off to church together. On our way back some young men were gathered in the square, sitting on culvert parapets and chewing the fat. Cripes was there. It seemed he had taken on an aura, a shot of courage that made him strut instead of walk, and speak intensely, not mumble. Proud of his return to the three R's. He gave me a warm wave of his arm.

12

Making progress

I was right about the change in Cripes. His head was held at a higher angle, as though he were looking into the distance to a goal. His eyes shone with a determined light and he held his arms straight, not dangling as before, with the fists slightly clenched. Nothing was going to stop him now.

He was even attending church, not the Anglican where my family and I worshipped, nor the Baptist, but the Church of God. He liked the camaraderie that existed at that denomination and the informal agenda of the service. He liked the jangle and rattle of the tambourine that accompanied the joyful singing of the hymns, and the way the congregation punctuated the sermons with generous helpings of 'Praise the Lord', 'Amen' and 'Hallelujah'. This milieu suited Cripes's personality to a T.

He was also gunning for the opportunity the church offered in the development of public speaking. Members could get up unafraid and unabashed and tell the congregation of their religious journey; of their past life, including sins, and of their present life, now sinless; of being lost and now saved. It was called testifying.

It was true that testifying made public speakers of even the very timid. I knew it to be true of Rusty Adams, a man who at one time covered his mouth with a hand to conceal the fact he had lost some teeth, while mumbling something to you. Now, since he had been testifying in the church, he had become a firebrand speaker, no longer covering his teeth-deficient mouth, and had not only emceed a few weddings but had also fought for the privilege to do so.

Cripes wanted that. He could read now, he could write, too, but he needed to improve his speech. I believe he must have testified a few times because, as you know, with practice comes perfection, or a stage near it. The fluency of his speech was improving and he was taking pains to speak correctly, too.

But rumour had it that one of the reasons he attended the church was not purely a religious one, or just a quest for oratory. Gossip had it that he had his eye on one of the sisters in the congregation. Sister? That's how members of the congregation address one another: Sister Roach, or Brother Cummings, as the case may be.

The apple of Cripes's eye was a Sister Rachel Anderson, a buxom twenty-year-old with full eyes, the voice of a bell and eyes as soft as a deer's.

I wished him well in his romance.

Cripes was not the only one who was progressing academically. I was too. My three mentors – Ma, Mr Dumfries and Mrs Quill – were seeing to it that I held a steady and constant course.

Ma smothered me with so many English exercises that I suspected she still had a hidden agenda that I would be so overwhelmed with work I would give up being on the farm and return to civilization, to her home. But if those were her motives, she didn't know this son of hers. I wasn't going to budge from my plan, and I was up to the challenge of the books, largely because I didn't spend too much time doing farm work now. Cripes, Alfred and the men Cripes hired bore the brunt of the work. My tasks had been whittled down to looking after the animals, which meant only morning and late-afternoon work. The rest of each day was mine to 'burn' the books.

Mr Dumfries was not sparing with the Geography assignments, either. From him I had many exercises involving map work, ordnance surveys and land utilization. On the syllabus were Physical Geography, Climate, Natural Vegetation, General World Geography and finally Regional Geography, for which I was studying the USA and Canada. In the exam itself there would be two papers of three hours duration each. There was quite a bit of work to do.

But if six hours of Geography exams seemed daunting, History was even more so. The prospectus was in three parts: English History, European History, and a special subject. I had chosen France under Louis XIV, 1661–1685. Of course I didn't have to do a huge sweep of English or European history. It would be too much. I had only to select one period in each. In the exam there would be three papers, each lasting three hours. Mercy!

Mrs Quill of course was my History mentor. She was a woman in her late fifties, wore glasses down on her nose, always had her hair in a tight bun and was a stickler for details. I had to write a paper every two weeks and include footnotes. But it was worth it.

From time to time I went up to the school in the afternoon, when the students had been dismissed, and discussed with Mrs Quill and Mr Dumfries anything I did not quite understand, and also to hand in and receive assignments. They were a great help.

I did not have a tutor for British Constitution. I was pretty much on my own. I tried to read the text as many times as I could. It was interesting reading, learning about the British monarchy, the House of Commons and House of Lords, the Cabinet, and so on. I learned what the name 'prime minister' meant: *primus inter pares*, first among equals. Taking exams is not only about passing them; it is also about learning interesting things.

From time to time Patrick Sugarman, Collie Rainer and Roy Darnell dropped by my place to chew the fat. They were school pals of mine, and they brought me news of school happenings – who was going out with whom, and so on.

I must admit that sometimes my heart skipped a beat. I was afraid to hear them say that one boy or another was taking an interest in Donna Rae. But time and time again I was spared the bad news. It seemed it was hands off that girl. Thank God for small mercies.

When I got tired of studying or doing assignments, I went for walks along the river. The countryside was restful on the eyes and calming to the brain. In the distance the trees were dense and blue and the red poinciana flowers that dotted their branches were like ribbons in a girl's hair. The water babbled over rocks here, eddied in a pool there and ran quietly at times. I would throw pebbles in the pool and watch the rings of water expand until they slammed into the banks. Those walks were relaxing.

If I meant to attain my objective of regaining Robin Hill and moving back up to the town, I had not only to think big, I had to act big.

Before he died my father had made an arrangement with Mrs Hilcher to lease her seventeen acres of land, which had been sitting idle since her husband had died. According to Mrs Hilcher the land was willed to Donna Rae, to do whatever she wanted with it when she attained the ripe age of twenty-one. I approached Mrs Hilcher and found that the arrangement to lease still stood – *if* I wanted the land. Of course I wanted it! So the deal was done.

'Bananas,' I told Cripes. 'We'll plant bananas.'

'I hear you, Rami,' he said with a grin. 'I hear you, sah.'

Now there's a thing about country folk. They like to savage the English language even when they know the correct word.

Cripes's use of 'sah' instead of 'sir' did not indicate he knew no better. 'Sah' just hit the spot more squarely for him.

Cripes hired four men to clear the land across the river from us, and we were on our way with the big expansion. We had the land ploughed and trenched to prevent erosion, and we decked the hills with bananas.

Soon I would be reaping a half a truckload of bananas weekly. Things were looking pretty good.

13

The garden party

It was summer. School was out. To raise funds to purchase new books the High School organized a garden party. I can't explain why this event went by that name because it had nothing whatsoever to do with a garden.

It was to be held on the school grounds, moving at night into the building. A dance in the gym would cap the day's festivities, and concessions were sold to vendors who would set up their stalls in other rooms throughout the school.

On the day itself a cricket team visited from a district named Withorn, and the match between them and our team was played on the local pitch. It was heart-tickling to hear the crack of the bat striking the ball and then to see the ball hurtling along the grass, or describing an arc to the boundary for a four-run hit or a six. At each crack of the bat the spectators responded with a rollicking cheer which seemed to hearten the batsman who had hit the ball.

Vendors were set up in several places and selling a variety of fares: ice-cold ginger beer, hot beef patties, curry goat with rice and a host of other things. Snowball was very popular – shaved ice topped with blood-red syrup, served in a glass. Children displayed to one another their syrup-reddened tongues. For them it was feast time. So much to eat, so much to drink.

In one area of the school grounds a chicken shoot attracted a troop of men, each parting with two shillings for the privilege of hitting a bull's-eye and winning the big roasted rooster. The gun cracked and cracked again before the shooter passed it to the next man. In the end Manny Randall carried the day. His shot penetrated the bull's-eye and he walked off with the rooster. Well, not walked exactly – a man like Manny Randall, Cripes's father, doesn't *walk* after a triumph like that. He strutted, much like the rooster he now held used to strut before the knife found its neck and the oven browned its flesh.

'I shoulda been a soldier,' he boasted. 'One shot an' I hit the bull's-eye. Muriel? Muriel?' he asked, searching the knot of mostly men. 'Whey's that dang woman? She missed seein' me win this 'ere bird.'

At about five in the afternoon the orchestra arrived from Lucea. No place in our small town, not even River Bottom, was out of earshot of the sweet melodies of the saxophone, trumpet and trombone as the band tuned up. It was going to be a night of dancing.

Cripes was busy polishing and shining his pair of black shoes. He had shaved and bathed.

'Going to the dance, Cripes?' I asked. Foolish question.

'Yes, sah,' he said.

'I thought your church didn't go in for such pleasures, Cripes.'

'Man no dead, no call him duppy,' he said, quoting one of the local proverbs.

I couldn't have put it any better myself. If he wasn't a ghost, why not live like a man?

'But,' I said, treading carefully, 'what if you gain a night of pleasure and lose the apple of your eye?'

'Apple of my eye?'

'You know – Sister Rachel.'

'Who told you about that, Rami?' he asked, smiling gratifyingly.

'Everybody knows you're sweet on her, Cripes. Don't deny it.'

'Well,' he said, grinning, 'I ain't ask her . . .'

'Ain't?' I interrupted.

'Oops,' he corrected. 'I mean I haven't asked her . . . nothing yet.'

I ignored his use of the double negative.

'So,' he finished, 'she can't hold it against me going to the dance. Perhaps I won't even dance, but I gotta be there. Listen to that sax bray man! I gotta be there.'

'That was much better talk you just did, Cripes. You're improving every day.'

'Because you're a strict teacher, Rami.'

'Thanks, Cripes. But I think your testifying at church has helped a lot.'

The night came and the school gym was full of revellers, men and women, even boys and girls. You see there were vendors selling all sorts of goodies. The children had helped to take the stuff there and, being there, were still helping out. But at times they wandered off, and the bravest and most talented boys would ask their chosen girl for her hand in dance and vie with the adults for floor space.

Donna Rae was there. Remember, her mother, Mrs Hilcher, was a baker. She was running one of the concessions that were set up in the classrooms. On her stall was an assortment of cakes, gizadas, drops, beef patties and coconut buns, known locally as toh-tohs. Her stall smelled of peppermint sticks – peppermint was another product she was capable of making.

Donna Rae and I exchanged pleasantries both with our eyes and with words. I nibbled on the stick of peppermint I had bought from her.

Ma and my sibs were there as well. Ma was a member of the committee that had put the garden party together, but now that her job was done, and everything was moving smoothly, she was ready to take her leave. I offered to buy the two sibs whatever they desired from Mrs Hilcher's stand,

and they opted for gizadas and peppermint sticks. Good choices, I thought.

They were snapping their fingers to the music so I said, 'How about a dance before you go?' I led them by the hand to the gym.

The band was a capable unit. The tenor sax reached down to the knee of its player, so long it was, and the trumpeter, perhaps imitating Louis Armstrong, held a white handkerchief in his left hand while he pumped the keys with the fingers of his right. The guitarist and trombonist completed the front row of musicians, while the drummer was in the rear. And oh, there was a woman on maracas at the back with the drummer. This was a progressive band – it was the first time I had seen a woman included in a band.

The three of us formed a circle and danced for a little while. My sibs had moves I was yet to learn and execute. Jolly good dancers they were. Ma looked on appreciatively. They grinned all the while they were dancing. I liked that. I had to give them as good as I was getting.

Eventually we hugged and said goodbye and the two imps winked at me in the light that shone from the overhead gas lamps.

Then the band struck up a three-part medley and the dancers went wild. Women, some of whom didn't seem able to crush an ant while walking, were now wild with ecstasy. Men had their arms stretched above their heads, the women, arms akimbo, matching them step for step and jiggle to jiggle: 'Rhumba, Rum and Cocoa-Cola and more rhumba'.

The music dug its way deep into the very soul of John Dinglewood, a softly-spoken man who now screamed with delight: 'Lord, what man a dead for?'

It was a revealing spectacle, a smorgasbord of personalities and human nature, pumped to the max by the enchanting music.

Seemingly avoiding the bright light, Cripes was in a shadowy corner. His felt hat was pulled low over his forehead. He was snapping his fingers to the beat of the music, but he wasn't dancing.

Brisk sales eventually eroded Mrs Hilcher's pile of goodies. Donna Rae took a breather, wandered off and straight into my arms.

The band, just as though we had requested it, slipped into that immortal tune, 'Sentimental Journey'. We slow-danced. Her breath on my neck was warm and peppermint-sweet, the tips of her fingers on my shoulder and upper arm as soft as powder puffs. Remember what happened to me the first time we kissed? That hot streak up and down my spine? Well, it was back. Zip, zip, wow! Zip, zip, wow!

I was in garden-party heaven.

14

Harvest

When Cripes returned from church services that Sunday, I asked him how he had fared with members of his church and particularly with his sweetheart.

'Were you bawled out for going to the dance?'

Cripes said the pastor had preached a sermon of fire and brimstone. He had chastised those who took pleasure in worldly things, forgetting to nurture their spiritual body. Cripes said the congregation had been fired up pretty good, too. He had never before heard them render so many 'Hallelujahs', 'Amens' and 'Praise-the-Lords'. He hadn't been personally reprimanded, he said, but he meant to toe the line from now on, because even in his sleep he was seeing the figure of Sister Rachel. 'Those big eyes, Rami, and those lips.'

The yams had reached maturity. The leaves had turned from rich olive-green to a faded-khaki look. It was time to dig them out, and what a harvest it turned out to be! The virgin land had done me proud. Three men, excluding Cripes, were digging some giants out of the hills. I measured a few of the biggest ones up against myself and some were up to knee-level, and a few got past there to my thigh. Such a crop!

Alfred and I carried them down to the roadside, and when I thought we had enough I stopped the men from digging. We would harvest the rest another day. Then we had a lunch of pepper-pot soup, made of salted beef, kale, okras and of course the freshly-dug negro yams. It was a satisfying meal.

Alfred harnessed the mules and hitched them to the cart, and the men loaded it full of yams. Alfred and I drove the cart up to the square and unloaded them. In all we made three trips.

Mr Rollington was a wholesaler from Green Island who bought yams, a truckload at a time if he could get them, and took them to Kingston where he sold them in the Coronation Market. When he saw my batch, he removed his glasses for a closer look.

'Boy, where'd you grow these monsters?'

'In a piece of virgin land, Mr Rollington.'

'They're just beautiful,' he said. 'The last time I saw yams like these was when Sun-Sun Johnson dug some beauties out of his farm. And that was a long time ago.'

'I am his son,' I said proudly.

He took a longer look at me. 'You don't say,' he commented. 'Golly me. I certainly won't have any trouble selling these.'

'I'll have more of the same next week.'

'Keep them coming,' he said encouragingly.

That batch weighed in at a little over two tons. I was in the money. I headed straight for the credit union.

That night Cripes and I sat at the table working out the pay for the men. I drew up a pay sheet. Cripes had been memorizing his times tables up to eight times. I wanted to test his multiplication skills.

'OK, Cripes,' I began, 'what do you make of this? How much is six times three shillings?'

'I don't know, Rami.'

'Are you saying you can't tell me how much you made today?'

'Sure I can. All I have to do is add four six times.'

As lead hand he made an extra shilling per hour.

'Yes, you could do that, but a headman will have to learn how to multiply. What if it was forty hours at three shillings, or four or five shillings?'

After thinking about what I had said for a few seconds he agreed with me: 'I see what you mean.'

Time and time again I had dangled the status of headman like a carrot before a donkey, and I am happy to say that worked every time for Cripes.

So we made a start with six times one.

'That's easy. Six.' Cripes replied.

'And six times two?'

On his face I could see that the gears of his brain were turning. After a few seconds, he shouted: 'Twelve.'

'Good, Cripes. Very good. Now six times three.'

And so, with some cajoling and encouragement he solved the problems. After we had converted shillings to pounds, using the formula twenty shillings to one pound sterling, the pay sheet looked like this:

Pay Sheet

Name	Hours and Rates	£	S	D
Cripes	6 hours @ 4 shillings per hour	1	4	0
Samson	6 hours @ 3 shillings per hour		18	0
Alfred	6 hours @ 3 shillings per hour		18	0
Bertie	6 hours @ 3 shillings per hour		18	0
	Total	3	18	0

Then, like a volcano that had been lying dormant, but was now rumbling and preparing to roar into life, Jake Hibbertson emerged again. Both of us had dug yams for Mr Rollington to buy. Jake's harvest of yams, piled like bricks in a wall, was across Main Street, opposite my own. A large haul it was, but clearly inferior to mine. It was obvious to me and to other experienced eyes that some had been dug out before they had reached maturity. Their lower tips showed a pale white where mature yams do not. Anyone would choose my lot over his, but in true Jake Hibbertson style he struck, letting greed triumph over common sense. Before I could get Mr Rollington to act on his promise to buy my yams, which he was still viewing with a light in his eyes, Jake ambled over, moving casually, but with a cat-that-was-about-to-swallow-the-canary smile etched across his face. When he took Mr Rollington aside and whispered to him, jerking his wicked head towards his pile, I smelled trouble.

Mr Rollington looked at my pile then back at Jake's. Finally he got into his truck and swung it over to the latter's and began to weigh and load the yams. He left me high and dry – with an estimated ton-and-a-half of yams unsold.

Jake had offered his yams at a cut rate – an astounding fifty per cent! As they say, money talks. Although Mr Rollington obviously preferred my yams, he was looking at the bottom line. And who could blame him?

As the truck drove off with his yams, Jake stood under his piazza, arms akimbo, looking over at me, gloating. He had outwitted the whippersnapper, yanked the rug from under me, or so he thought.

For a long while I didn't know what to do. So many yams, and no market for them. Neither the Green Island nor the Grange Hill market and alas not even the Sav-la-mar market were big enough to absorb so many giants. Alfred, Cripes and I sat down, dumbfounded. They took turns cursing Jake, then consoling me; cursing him some more and again assuring me of my resilience. I was left in deep thought. And then I got it.

The Brown's Town market lay far away on the north coast of the island, past Lucea and Montego Bay, in the parish of St Ann. I knew a roving truckman who took sellers there. He came through on Friday evenings. So to Brown's Town I would go, and I'd take Cripes along.

At Brown's Town I did indeed manage to sell most of my yams wholesale to higglers, one hundredweight here, two there. They'd do retail. I had little time for too much of that. I didn't make quite as much money as I would have had Mr Rollington bought my yams, but at least I saved the harvest.

When I got back, I couldn't tell who Ma was more angry with, me or Jake. She just couldn't absorb the notion that her son, though not a little boy anymore, could venture so far from home to sell and haggle like any other marketgoer. But when I reminded her that in no way would I allow Jake to triumph, she knew in her heart I'd done the right thing.

'Don't tell me you mean to do this until all the yams are sold!'

'If I have to, Ma.'

She almost tore her hair out. 'Oh, God, hear my prayer.'

But I didn't have to go back to the Brown's Town market. Applying caution and a wait-and-see attitude, I didn't dig out any yams the following week. I wanted to see what would develop.

I was sitting on my verandah, reading a chapter of *Louis XIV of France*, when Wally Timberlane, a roustabout, came running down the road. Mr Rollington had sent him, he gasped, out of breath. Could I come up and see him?

'Why?' I asked.

Wally didn't know. I was curious, so I went.

Mr Rollington was apologetic. Sorry he had left me in the lurch last week, he said. He had let greed get in the way of good business judgement. Lost money on Jake's yams, he admitted. Not a good lot, he said, not an easy sell. Well, the long and short of it was that he implored me to provide him with a two-ton dig of good yams in the coming week. Two tons, three even, whatever I could manage.

'And you won't dish me dirt again, Mr Rollington?'

'No dirt, young Johnson. I promise. Scout's honour.'

So we shook on it. I was back in business.

The following week I dug up a good batch of yams, and Mr Rollington was true to his word, scout's honour and all. He snapped up the lot, which weighed in at a couple of hundred-weights under two tons.

Jake was standing under his piazza again, but he didn't walk across to have a tête-à-tête with Mr Rollington on that day. He just stood there steaming at the notion that quality had won the day.

Mr Rollington didn't totally ignore Jake's harvest, but he picked through it carefully, taking only the ones he considered would meet market demand. So Jake was the one who was left with about half of his dig lying on the side of the street. To needle him I gave a V sign in his direction, and Cripes rubbed it in when he tossed his cap in the air.

I had carried the day, but what would Jake do next? I would have to wait and see.

15
Hit the road, Jake

The following week we dug the last of the yams out, huge ones again, a final two tons less a hundredweight. For me it was more money in the credit union.

Yams are annuals. After they are reaped, the field dies. The farmer moves on to a fresh plot, leaving the old one to restock itself with nutrients. Not so bananas. The field perpetuates itself. Around the parent plant pop out young shoots or suckers. The smallest ones are dug out and planted elsewhere, thereby increasing the size of the field. The largest shoot remains with the parent plant and when the latter produces fruit and is chopped down, this shoot takes its place. So there is a constant stream of fruit through the years.

The bananas on the Hilcher lease were growing speedily, anxious to bear fruit. My credit rating at the credit union had been given a big boost by the sale of the yams, and the weekly sale of bananas was adding to it. My plans were gelling nicely.

Time has a way of weeding out ideas, leaving only the worthwhile ones in place. So it was with my original plans for a store. Now I could see that a store would only suck away my time and energy and get in the way of expanding my fields. The latter needed only my supervisory time; the store would need too much of my attention.

Managed by Cripes, the farm would not only be productive it would grow in acreage, which would fall right in with my plans. I needed a steady income for achieving my main goal: Robin Hill. And that prize seemed well within my grasp.

Jake Hibbertson was no longer the tough rival he could have been. Since about the time that Cripes had thrown in his lot with me, I had gained strength and he had lost some of the fight in him. As he poured bottle after bottle of rum into his body, his fortunes slipped away from him. His store had empty shelves, and his farm produced not only less and less but poorer quality crops.

He had gradually lost the respect of the community. When he first ousted my father from Robin Hill, the townsfolk saw him as a shrewd businessman, not a cut-throat. If at first he had seemed to have taken on the aura of a Robin Hood in outwitting the rich, he now appeared to be lacking the talent for giving to the poor. After my father had given his life to save him from the fire, the level of people's adulation of him had taken a big dip. They began to see him as an opportunist who had dethroned Father, not so much for advancement as for spite.

My growing success rattled him. The father had been destroyed, but through his son, that father had risen from the ashes like a phoenix to haunt him.

There was a rumour that he meant to pull up sticks, move along and rebuild in Sav-la-mar. He was through with farms, the rumour said, through too with small-fry stores. In Sav he would go into big business – a department store or hardware emporium.

The rumour heartened me. If he sold out, wouldn't I be ready to purchase Robin Hill? You bet. But would he sell it to me? That I doubted. I would have to use tact.

When I learned he had engaged the services of a realtor, I shouted two hallelujahs because it would better my chances. If Jake would not sell to me, the realtor might. Then I heard that his store and his pasture abutting River Bottom were both sold. However it seemed that Jake had left town before he had sold all his property. What good news! No more would I have to worry about his dirty tricks and – the real bonus – Robin Hill could soon be mine.

But if Jake couldn't have a last hurrah, he wouldn't be Jake. He had left town, but he had prescribed a poison pill. On no account was Robin Hill to fall into my hands. When I approached the realtor, he began to hem and haw. Then there were questions, and more questions. Did I have the means? Would I be able to land a mortgage? Why was I interested in purchasing that particular piece of real estate?

All his questions were answered, even though they were none of his business.

I had the indirect support of many of the townsfolk – none of them would put in an offer for the land themselves. They thought it was rightfully mine, wrested from the Johnson clan by a sly and merciless Jake.

It was time to execute a detour around Mr Realtor. With the help of Frank Billet, Father's good friend and now my confidante, we planned a coup. He fronted for me. He put in a bid for the property and placed a down payment on it, my money of course, as though he were buying it himself. And the realtor took the bait. The credit union was in on the caper, too. I negotiated a mortgage with them, and the property the realtor thought he was selling to Mr Billet was really being sold to me – a perfectly executed *coup d'état*.

Once again Robin Hill was Johnson property!

I have a special place in my memory for the first time I set foot on Robin Hill as the owner of the property. It was a breezy day. The Trade Winds were in a jolly mood, swinging tree branches about and fluttering small leaves, bending the trunks of tall coconut trees. John Crows, those venerable vultures, and other birds floated and banked on the warm currents.

I wasn't afraid to return to the place where I was born and where I had spent my happy childhood years, but as I ascended the hill, my heart began to thump like a drum.

As I walked through the charred remains and visited each room, I said to myself: This was the living room and this the kitchen . . . This was my room . . ., and so on. Gradually my heart stopped its wild pounding and I felt much calmer by the time I had completed my walk around what remained of the house, but I must admit I felt humble.

I sat on the stone steps, which were still intact, and looked at the town below me. I had done this many a time. The view was much the same, except that there were many new houses where there used to be empty lots. A feeling of accomplishment flooded my body and I basked in the hope that some time in the near future I would be back to stay and be able to look down on the town every day. As I left I spoke aloud to the blackened walls: 'I shall return,' I promised.

16

Examinations

Donna Rae had dropped out of studying for the GCE O Level English. She was in the fifth form and was gunning for the Higher Schools Certificate Examination instead. Whatever else she had had her mind set on as a career she had abandoned that. She knew she would get by without the GCE English. The career she had chosen was teaching and the Higher Schools Certificate was enough to launch her on this course.

She seemed to have the idea in her head that Ma harboured a mindset that no local girl was a worthy catch for me, so she, Donna Rae, was determined to take up teaching. She would return to us, a local girl, but an educated, career one. Ma would see. She would be worthy.

None of this was discussed with me, however, I just knew it.

Meanwhile I was eager to see how much Cripes had improved. I had not thrown out Cripes's first attempt at writing about the mango tree in our yard. The mistakes had been underlined in red, but that was all. One day I pulled it out and handed it to him.

As he read it his eyes opened wider and his mouth fell open. 'I wrote that?'

I nodded.

He blurted out one of our milder expletives: 'Rawtid! It's very bad.'

I told him I'd like him to rewrite the passage, spelling the words correctly if he could, paying attention to punctuation but not changing the gist of the paragraph. This he did, and this was the new version:

> *The mango tree is big. It is taller than the house. It has plenty of branches and leaves. The tree has blossoms and bees are flying round the blossoms. One day it will bear mangos. They come out small. Small like cashoo nuts. They are green. They grow green ~~untill~~ until they get ripe then they turn yellow and red like Miss Tailor's ~~cheicks~~ cheeks, Heh! Ripe mango is sweet, green mango is sower, I like mangos.*

Still some spelling mistakes and other errors, but wasn't that an improvement!

I shook his hand. 'It's much better, Cripes. You've come a long way, man.'

He grinned. He was going places. And what with his giving testimony at his church, his speech was a hundred per cent better. The power of public speaking and a woman's love – oops! prospective love – had worked wonders.

Donna Rae sat for and passed the Higher Schools Certificate exam. I was right behind her. In the summer of 1956 I went to Kingston and sat for my GCEs. In the autumn of the same year I went back and did the British Constitution exam. When the results came back I had aced Geography, History and English with distinctions, but in British Constitution I had managed only a pass. Still, not bad for a dropout.

I bought thank-you gifts for Mr Dumfries and Mrs Quill: a book of photography for that kind gentleman, whom I had learned had just taken up the hobby, and for gracious Mrs Quill a desk set accompanied by a bouquet. For her efforts in tutoring me in English, Ma had to settle for a big kiss on the cheek. Mothers don't mind, anyway.

I told Ma I was ready to move on. 'I've succeeded in doing what I set out to do. The fields are doing fine. My small plots of yams and bananas are now big fields, the banana field particularly. Every week I put about half a truckload of bananas on the roadside to be graded and picked up. Money is rolling in, and once again Robin Hill is in Johnson hands.'

She hugged me tight and began to cry. Something in the moment touched me, and then I too was shedding tears and feeling no shame whatsoever. It felt like a reprieve, as if a load had been cut loose from my shoulders.

'Now what?' she asked.

'I've applied to the university. If I'm accepted, I'll be starting next semester.'

More hugs but no more tears.

'And what about the fields? Are you going to sell out?'

'Sell? No way. Cripes will be managing the farm while I'm away.'

'What? Cripes? Have you lost your mind?'

'No, Ma. Cripes can handle it. He's grown not only intellectually but responsibly as well. Ma, I feel so jolly good that I've turned a functionally illiterate man into a viable individual.'

'That's all good, but can you entrust your money to him?'

'I could and I would if you weren't here. So that's where you come in.'

'Me? Come in where?'

'I'm asking you to be the banker, Ma. Cripes will give out the work – fields to be weeded, yams to be planted, tended and harvested, bananas to be cut down and sold. He'll make up the hours and pay-outs, but you'll take care of the money – bank it and withdraw it to pay the workers. But, and I can't emphasize it enough, *Cripes* will pay the workers. He'll make up the pay sheet and tell you what each worker's wage is, and he'll pay them. Let him have that responsibility. He's doing that now. Don't take it away from him.'

'You know, Rami, you put me to shame. Here I am, the adult, and I'm learning from you. I'll have to come down from my high horse and begin to see the good in people, if there is good, irrespective of their status. Thank you, my son.' She paused. 'So you've lived your dream.'

'Actually it was Father's dream. He died before he could fulfil it. I couldn't let Jake win with people thinking of us as losers. Now I'll pursue my dream.'

'And if you're accepted in university, what course do you plan to pursue?'

'Arts, of course. I'm thinking of majoring in either Geography or History. In time I'll decide which. I love them both.'

'And after graduation – assuming you will graduate?'

'There's no *if* here, Ma. I *will* graduate. And hopefully I'll come back here to teach.'

'Rami!' she beamed. 'Another teacher in the family. Go get that degree, Tiger.'

Another hug, a rather long one.

'So,' she said, 'I offered no help while you were living your father's dream, as you put it. I didn't want to interfere. But now that you are embarking on yours, I'd like to be a part of it. I'll pay your tuition fees at the university. Any objections?'

'None whatsoever, Ma.'

Mothers! Aren't they the best?

'I can't get over the fact that you started out on this quest aged seventeen, and you have accomplished so much. A thousand congratulations, son.'

'Thanks, Ma. It wasn't easy, but something like rage drove me on.'

'If you rebuild Robin Hill, you'll have come full circle.'

'It will be rebuilt, Ma.'

'A big house?'

'Oh yes. Big enough for a family of six, perhaps.'

Ma's pretty mouth fell open. 'Do you mean . . . ?'

I laughed and winked at her. 'A boy turns into a man and eventually, if he's up to it, he marries, Ma.'

'That girl?'

I played dumb. 'What girl?'

'Don't dodge the question, Rami. You know who I mean.'

'Oh, that girl!'

Brad and Arlene giggled. They have always found any discussion that involved Donna Rae titillating stuff. Imps.

I didn't answer Ma. After all only death and taxes, and the sun rising each and every day are certain. I left her on the hook. She said she had changed and was ready to see people from the inside so she wouldn't be stewing. Only waiting.

From where I was standing the future looked jolly good.

17

Harvest Sunday

Every year in October one Sunday was set aside by our Anglican Church for Harvest Festival. On such a Sunday the congregation made offerings to the church, and not just anything, but the best in crops, the fattest animals, the most scrumptious baked goods, ready-made clothing and even embroidery work.

The church was literally overflowing with offerings. Heaped in front of the altar and around the walls were yams, avocados, bunches of bananas and plantains, coconuts, pumpkins, pineapples and squashes. Sugar canes, big ones called bamboo canes because of their length and size, were draped on either side of each window. Their leaves, still attached, were entwined in the centre to form leafy arches. They not only added colour to the church but they were also a great treat to eat later.

There were flowers too, roses and lilies.

It was a colourful church and the congregation was fresh and eager for a rousing service. A pleasant aroma of khus-khus-scented clothing swirled around the church. The ribbons in the children's hair dotted the congregation like flowers and white feathers enlivened what were otherwise drab hats. There were hats trimmed with baubles, hats with wide brims and some with no brims, like fezzes. The men were hatless, of course, and they had taken great care to plaster their hair with pomade and enough brilliantine to make it glisten in the sunlight which streamed through the open windows.

The bell-ringer was smashing the tong against the bell and the sound of the stricken instrument reverberated over the hills. The service was about to commence.

I was one of seven surplice boys. We all wore white gowns over our clothes. Assembling in the vestry, we led the minister up the aisle to the altar. The lead boy carried an ornamental cross, the rest of us walked two abreast. The minister brought up the rear. He held his Bible and hymnal very piously close to his chest. As we tunnelled our way up the aisle, the congregation sang:

> All things bright and beautiful,
> All creatures great and small,
> All things wise and wonderful,
> The Lord God made them all.

As I went by the pew my family sat in, I winked at Brad and Arlene, and, as on other Sundays, they winked back. Arlene was a much better winker than Brad, but, no matter, all three of us enjoyed our little sideshow, which we indulged in every Sunday.

The Rev. Ledbetter was in the middle of leading the congregation in prayer, when two gentlemen entered the church – Mr Caleb Briggs and Mr Josiah Carrier. Ordinarily when anyone arrived after the service had begun, that person entered through the vestry, thereby minimizing any commotion. But these two chose instead to enter through the main door.

Briggs was a well-built old gentleman, and Carrier was likewise old but thinner. They caused enough disruption to force the minister to suspend prayers in midstream, because as they walked, their shoes squeaked like rats. *Crips, crips, crips.* Almost topping that was the scent of mothballs emanating from their clothes, which hit the congregation in a wave. Their entrance provoked stifled laughter among the congregation. When these venerable gentlemen were finally settled in their seats, the Rev. Ledbetter finished the prayer.

Later he preached a brilliant and energetic sermon, the theme of which was 'giving'. He praised the congregation for their generous gifts to the House of the Lord and suggested that their giving should not be confined to this one day in the year but should be a gesture practised all year round; that not only God should be remembered with gifts but the poor, the lame and the sick as well.

After an hour we were all happy to escape the heat of the church for the breezy outdoors, where the congregation always took time to socialize.

Donna Rae and I found and greeted each other.

'Girl, you look so beautiful,' I said. Of course she blushed. But it was true. Her beauty grew right along with her maturity. Her skin was immaculate and fresh. 'What do you do with all the time you've got since the pressure of studying has passed?'

'Oh, I'm biding my time. I read, I help Ma. Such things.'

'Yes, I'm enjoying the hiatus, too. But d'you know what I miss since we've stopped studying together? Our kiss.'

Again Donna Rae blushed.

Brad and Arlene found me, and, one on either side of me, clung on to me. Then Ma was coming our way, and Donna Rae decided to take her leave. As she walked away her milk-white skirt swirled around her knees. Beauty, grace and purity – that was Donna Rae.

Ma didn't waste any time. 'So you're serious about that girl, are you?'

'Ma,' I said, 'a man doesn't show his hand to another woman. You know that.'

'I'm not another woman. I'm your loving mother. I want to know what your intentions are.'

In a singsong voice my sibs got into the act. 'Rami has a girlfriend. Rami has a girlfriend . . .'

Ma stomped a patent-leathered foot. 'Children, stop that!'

With hands covering their mouths, they stifled their merriment.

'Wasn't that a great service, Ma? Didn't the Reverend let it loose today?'

'Don't change the subject, young man! What are your intentions towards that girl?'

'Her name is Donna Rae, Ma. You know that.'

'OK,' she conceded, 'Donna Rae. What are your intentions towards her?'

In a gesture of tomfoolery I turned my eyes towards the ocean-blue sky. For a moment. Just for a moment.

Then I began: 'My intentions, my intentions. I intend to enter the University of the West Indies – if of course I'm accepted . . .' I was rattling it off at top speed now. 'During this time I intend to keep in touch with Donna Rae. What are good friends for if not to keep the fires burning? And after graduation, a job right here at the High School, if of course there's a vacancy. There'd better be one. And maybe, and it's a strong maybe, marriage. How about that for intent, Ma?'

She couldn't stand it. 'Boy, you're trying my patience.'

'Have you forgotten that we discussed this before? That when Robin Hill is rebuilt, there will be the little feet of children pitter-pattering all over the place? The only blind spot is which girl will be their mother. Ma, you are breaking your promise. D'you remember you said you would come off your high horse and evaluate people for their inner self? Your questions reveal you still have a problem with Donna Rae.'

In her face I could spot regret, and also an attempt to get down off her high horse.

'Arlene, Brad,' she said, 'let's go. Say 'bye to your brother. OK, Rami.'

My sibs had enjoyed every bit of the drama. Before they left they winked their satisfaction at me. So cute those two. So blissfully cute.

I was joined by the Randalls, Cripes's parents.

Mr Randall was dressed in a dark-blue striped suit and a hat that was too big for his head. I could only assume that when he tried it on and the salesman commented the hat was too big, he took it anyway, simply because he was too stubborn to let anyone interfere in his decision-making. If you remember how his son got his unfortunate name, you'll agree that my assumption was probably correct. The hat rested on his ears and almost concealed his eyes, but he tilted it back now, the better to see me.

Mrs Randall, a rather shy woman, was wearing a green dress and matching hat that was more artificial flowers than hat.

'Hello, young Johnson,' Mr Randall said, extending his hand. We shook. Mrs Randall followed suit and shook my hand, too.

'I like what you doin' for my boy, young Johnson.'

'Yes, yes,' parroted Mrs Randall, 'you treatin' him real good.'

'I try my best,' I told them. 'After all he's done well for me. He's great company and we look out for each other.'

'I get your meanin',' Mr Randall said. 'I like your style. I heard 'bout Hibbertson an' his move 'gainst you. If my boy had carried out Hibbertson's dirty work, I woulda whupped him myself. But good he hooked up wit' you instead. I like what I see in 'im. Boy's got a light in 'is eyes. Struts like a rooster in a hen house. You put sand in his craw, young Johnson. 'E's a chip off the ol' block, ain't he, Muriel? Jus' like me when I was courtin' you.'

'So you say, Manny.'

'So you say, so you say. What's wrong with you, woman?' He chuckled, then continued, 'Boy's even goin' to church. 'E's got courage to spare. Prob'ly soon get married, an' I owe it all to you, young Johnson.' He turned to his wife. 'Don't you think he done right goin' after that young heifer of a Sister Anderson, Muriel?'

Mrs Randall was certainly not as enthusiastic as her husband that her only son might be contemplating marriage. 'Whatever you say, Manny.'

'What you mean by "whatever I say", woman?' stormed the man, who was convinced he wore both the pants and the dress in his family. 'Can't you say somethin' original?'

Mrs Randall took up the challenge. 'Cripes is even readin' newspaper now,' she said, 'and books. Never seen him do that before.'

It was true. Ever since he had crawled out of the morass of semi-illiteracy, Cripes had become an avid reader. He read all the books I borrowed from Arlene and Brad. If he saw a scrap of paper on the roadway while he was out walking, Cripes would pick it up and read it. It mattered not what the subject was, be it part of a story, a newspaper article or even an advertisement. Once or twice I saw him reading, or trying to read, my textbooks.

Manny consulted his fob watch. 'Young man,' he said to me, 'we've got to run. Muriel has to cook dinner. Ain't you, Muriel?'

Mrs Randall was back to what seemed her standard answer: 'So you say, Manny.'

'Dang woman,' Manny said under his breath.

We shook hands and they ambled away.

Messrs Briggs and Carrier had finished socializing and were ready to head home. Their mounts were patiently waiting, swishing their tails though there were no flies. Briggs rode a nag, Carrier a mule. Both animals had small coils of rope attached to their saddles. No one know why the two old codgers carried the ropes. Obviously they had no intention of lassoing any animal, certainly not while they were dressed in their Sunday best. Perhaps they had adopted the practice after they had seen a western movie and liked the idea of living vicariously as cowboys.

The following day, Monday, was sale day for the harvest offerings. The ground produce was brought out into the yard, and a mountain of it there was, too. Tables were set up and were heaped with baked goods of every description. The list was long, the goodies varied.

Animals that couldn't have been brought to the church on Sunday were there now – goats, fat pigs and poultry – all making bleating, oinking and clucking noises. There were two heifers and a donkey cub for sale, too.

Women crowded around the ready-made clothes and the hand-embroidered blouses, skirts and place mats.

All in all there was a happy troop of buyers, including some from neighbouring villages. Some had come to purchase things for their own use, while others intended to resell them in the Wednesday markets at Green Island or at Grange Hill.

Mrs Hilcher was present, and Donna Rae was along to help. To remain close to her I offered to help them with their stall.

The Rev. Ledbetter mingled. He was dressed casually in khaki, but he still wore his white collar.

Mr Canista, a sort of animal broker, arrived in his mule-drawn cart. He bought animals, kept them for a while, fattening those which needed more flesh, then reselling them at a profit. He bought four shoats and three goats and loaded them into his cart. He was the most prolific spitter anyone in our town had ever known. He spat minute by clockwork minute. No one could figure out how his glands were able to produce so much saliva non-stop. Actually he had started out as a butcher, but he lost customers who wondered where he was spitting with the meat all around him. Of course everybody at the sale was happy to see him drive off with his purchases, because while he remained, no one would eat with all that spitting going on.

18

Cripes comes of age

Cripes was now courting Sister Rachel and, from his upbeat attitude and keen attention to hygiene, he was making progress. When he suggested that we paint the house, I was all for it. After all, while I was away at university, he would be living there, not free of course, but for a nominal rent. I wasn't about to make the mistakes my father had made. One should embellish one's actions with kindness, but it should not become a substitute for action.

So we not only painted the house but we nailed a new zinc roof on and it looked pretty good, fit for a bride.

One evening Cripes returned from visiting Sister Rachel, and he was beaming like a beacon. All of his teeth were showing gleaming white and even his eyes seemed to be laughing.

'Rami, I popped the question,' he chortled like a child who had just completed a complicated puzzle.

'And?' I asked.

'She said yes. Her parents said yes. Yes, yes, *yes*!' He slapped his thighs as loud as a thunderclap.

I was happy for him and shook his hands. 'Congratulations, Cripes.'

'Thank you, man. I owe it all to you, Rami.'

'No, no. I did a little but . . .'

'Yes, Rami, It's you. *You* taught me how to read, to write and do 'rithmetic. You gave me the courage to . . . you know

. . . spread my wings. You gave me a position on the farm and that makes me look good and feel good.'

'OK,' I said. 'I was happy to help with the schooling, but you had it in you all along.'

His happiness lasted for weeks.

One Saturday it rained from morning till noon. Cripes and a few young men decided to go crab-hunting in a mangrove swamp in Green Island. He asked me if I wanted to go along.

'Why not?' I said. I had so much free time to use up, and I had never been on such a hunt.

Green Island is a town west of us, built in two parts. At the time I am writing, the eastern part boasts the police station, court house, Public Works Department, the large Anglican church and some residences. The western section, where stand the business places, lies at the end of a curving sea coast, which has a mangrove swamp behind it.

The heavy rain had flooded the holes where the crabs lived, forcing them to seek whatever dry ground was left to them, or to climb up onto the mangrove trees. Thus exposed, with very few places to skitter, we were able to scoop them up and put them into our crocus bags.

At about two in the morning we returned, most of us with our bags three-quarters full. My bag was only half full, but it was enough. Cripes and I had crabs for Sunday breakfast. It was sweet fun cracking open the big claws of the males and scooping out the tasty white flesh. The females were prized for their fatness. It was a fine breakfast.

Cripes strung some of the nicer ones on a cord and took them up to his fiancée. I did likewise and took a batch of fifteen up to Ma's.

Arlene and Brand could scarcely contain their excitement. If they had had their own way, they would have skipped church. In no simple terms they warned Fantasia not to cook the crabs before they returned from church. They wanted to see the crabs' reaction as they were dunked into the steaming pot. Sadists! Brad went so far as to threaten her with perpetual damnation in hell if she failed to comply. He backed up his threat by informing Fantasia of his close alliance with the Rev. Ledbetter, who in turn had connections both in the Kingdom of Heaven and the Republic of Hell, and any slip-up on her part would certainly gain her a disastrous existence in purgatory. Fantasia acceded. With such a threat who wouldn't?

With time on my hands and, using Ma's car, I learned to drive, and eventually got my driver's licence, which for any young man, is a prized possession.

I bought a pith helmet, which would be passed on to Cripes when I went to university. But once in a while I went uptown, wearing the helmet and riding Lizette. I still couldn't forget the jeers and the pinpricks I had felt on the day Father and I had left Robin Hill and passed through the square; those people standing under the shops' piazzas, laughing at us; my father riding on a cart and not driving the truck he once owned; me riding the mule bareback.

Now I was riding the same mule, this time saddled, and wearing the pith helmet. Now they were referring to me as Busha Rami – 'busha' meaning overseer. In their eyes I had come full circle.

Very little had changed. As the saying goes, 'money talks'. When my father was considered a bigwig, he was respected. He was Busha Sun-Sun, but when he lost his money, the respect evaporated. It was transferred to Jake Hibbertson. He became the Big Kahuna. Then when he began to slip, it was Drunkard Jake.

Now it was my turn. I had come up from River Bottom. I was still there, but figuratively I had come up. Now I was being showered with respect. Busha Rami! Give me a break. Can't a person just be respected for his or her qualities? My father had stumbled, but he was still Sun-Sun Johnson. A kind man, a selfless man, always giving, to the point of giving his life. Yet they had failed to see that. Only after he had made the supreme sacrifice in the fire that night had some respect filtered back to him.

I felt gratified not only for myself but for Cripes Randall as well. He had learned to read, to write and do arithmetic. Now he was proud and he too was getting respect.

19

Interlude

I was enjoying the interlude before I began university, and what a feeling of relief washed over me. A burden had fallen away. My body felt light and elastic. Now I was catching up with life around me and my senses drank in the wonders of the natural world.

Once again I became aware of the scent of flowers and the noise of bees buzzing among them. Lizards caught my eye as they ran down one tree trunk and skittered across the grass to run up another. I saw their green-brown bodies as things bright and beautiful, just as we had sung in the hymn – 'All things bright and beautiful, the Lord God made them all'. Marigolds, which to me had always been mundane weeds, were now a poetic yellow in the jigsaw of nature. And those frogs in the nearby river, ribbeting love songs in their bassoon voices, sounded like an opera to me. Fireflies, commonly seen and ignored, now appeared as master craftsmen, stringing broken wires of gold on the dark canvas of the night. The hoots of owls registered with me as questions, Who? Who? Who? as they bridged the gap between the darkened hills.

Thunder was always with us, pretty mundane stuff, but now, in flights of fancy, I thought someone was up there knocking over chairs. And the rain that usually follows – how many times had I sat on the verandah and seen it stream down? But now it wasn't just water hitting the earth, it was the clouds stitching the earth with silver threads of water. There was poetry everywhere and my senses in their heightened state of awareness appreciated it to the full. A boy who had become a man before he was ready was alive again.

I picked some weeds, hardly thicker than threads, which some call love weed. I threw them in the air and asked, 'Who is my true love?' As if I didn't know. The weed could not have had a more appropriate name. It was the most durable and tenacious plant I know. Throw it anywhere, on the driest, most barren soil and it doesn't merely survive, it grows, like love. Two weeks later I passed where I had thrown them and noticed they had not only taken root but multiplied.

I let Cripes run the show at River Bottom. He was getting the feel of management duties and loving it.

It gave me time to pick up a game of cricket with the boys. 'Hey, Rami, want to bowl?' Sure I wanted to. Not so good at batting, I was however a formidable bowler. *Pow* – the sound of the bat connecting with the ball. *Splat* – my breaking ball knocking the wickets down – one batsman out.

I went to the square on Friday nights – as I had done countless times before – but now I went as a hedonist. Friday nights were nothing less than mini-carnivals in the square. Just about everybody was there. Friday, being payday, meant most had money to spend. The older people were in the stores, the women making purchases, the men slamming down dominoes, or sipping cold beer, or rum and Coca-Cola. The street belonged to the young. It was not unusual for someone to start plucking a banjo or strumming a guitar and for a third to add bass with a rumba box. Many a time an impromptu dance began right there in the street to such tunes as 'You are my sunshine, my only sunshine' or 'Brown skin gal stay home and mind baby'. Some romances blossomed right there on Friday nights. Sometimes a truck or a car came by, blaring its horn or bisecting the crowd with its cones of light in much the same way as Moses allegedly did to the Red Sea.

Fantastic nights, glorious times. And to think I had had to miss out on them for so long. I was there, Cripes was there, and Alfred too.

Alfred still worked for me. He was not the same, though. Never a jolly man or a talkative one, he was noticeably quieter now. He was obviously peeved by Cripes's rise to prominence. First Cripes had moved in with me, an unheard of breach of social practice. Not even Sun-Sun Johnson, my easygoing father, would have broken the code – so thought Alfred, my mother and a host of others.

But for me it was different. I needed Cripes. I had needed his muscle in case Jake had sent more troublemakers down to River Bottom. Cripes had nowhere to stay, and why should Alfred mind anyway? He had his own home.

The further advancement of Cripes to the position of headman nettled Alfred immensely. But I couldn't have given him the position. As far as I knew Alfred hadn't got very far in school, and he must have been sixty or thereabouts in age. I needed a younger man who could grow with the farm.

One day things came to a head when Cripes told him to fill a barrel with water so they could commence spraying the banana fields.

'Who you orderin'?' snapped Alfred. 'I is a bigger man than you!'

'Well, Alfred,' countered Cripes. 'You're certainly older than me, but I just doing my job.'

'A hurry-come-up, that's what you is,' fumed Alfred.

'Take it easy, Alfred. Don't go calling me names.' Cripes was trying to keep a lid on the blow-up.

I stepped in. 'Alfred,' I began, 'Cripes got the position of headman because he earned it. He can read, write and make calculations on paper.'

'I can sign my name,' Alfred pointed out.

'Yes, yes,' I said, 'but it takes more than being able to sign your name.' I showed him a pay sheet and the calculations that were on it.

He shook his head a few times before he said, 'I see what you mean.' But wagging a finger, he admonished Cripes: 'Jus' don' order me aroun'.'

And that was that.

20

Two graduations and a wedding

Donna Rae and I left for Kingston the same time, she to Shortwood Teachers' Training College and I to the Mona Campus of the University of the West Indies. We weren't too far apart, and we kept in close touch. When we weren't talking on the telephone, we went on dates which took us to flower-rich, picnic-friendly, romance-inducing Hope Gardens, or to a movie at the Carib Cinema at Cross Roads. We often topped off such movie outings with two piping-hot Bruce's beef patties, bought in the Cross Roads area as well.

Students who entered teachers' training colleges with passes in the Third Jamaica Local Exam had to undergo training in methodology and classroom management, do practice teaching, plus three years of rigorous academic upgrading as well. Donna Rae's situation was different. She was accepted into the programme on the basis of her pass in the Higher Schools Certificate and graduated after one year.

Armed with her Teachers' Certificate she returned to our town and was promptly taken onto the staff of the elementary school.

That was unfortunate for me since I still had two years before I would graduate. We were now miles apart. Letter writing helped, but it just couldn't bridge the gap. So I remedied it by buying a used car. It enabled me to pay regular weekend visits home, not only to see Donna Rae, but to check on the farm and make sure that Cripes was doing a good job. And he was. Everything looked shipshape. My credit union account, depleted by the purchase of Robin Hill, was once again growing.

At the end of my first year in university, Cripes tied the knot with Sister Rachel. One could scarcely believe that the once rough-and-tumble Cripes could look so debonair, standing at the altar awaiting his bride-to-be. His razor-thin moustache and fine haircut complemented to a T his grey suit, and red cummerbund.

Sister Rachel was no less enthralling in her white dress and veil as she advanced up the aisle in that quasi-military march that brides do. It was difficult to tell who was more proud to see her, Cripes or his father.

True to his nature, Manny Randall nearly caused a ruckus at the reception that followed. He stood up and boldly usurped the floor from the master of ceremonies. He objected that church regulations had substituted fruit punch for wine. He said that a marriage in the Anglican church was toasted with wine not fruit punch. His argument was based on the story of the wedding at Cana in Galilee, John, chapter two. As he put it: When the party ran out of wine, didn't Jesus ask for waterpots to be filled with water which He turned into wine? Wasn't it because Christ was convinced that a wedding without wine was akin to having a carriage without a horse? If people are now turning their backs on the tradition of toasting with glasses of wine, isn't that in fact being disrespectful to Christ's own behaviour?' Then defiantly, he went on to reach under the table and pull a bottle of red wine out of a bag. He poured himself a glass, raised it, saying, 'Drink a toast wit' me. To Christ!'

He drank and we drank – he the red wine and we the fruit punch.

Quickly he refilled his glass. 'Now,' he continued with a grin, 'a toast to my son who has rosed from the depths in leaps an' bounds to bag his pretty bride, the belle o' the town.' He raised the glass of red. 'To my son, Cripes Randall.'

He drank and we drank.

Nobody protested except his wife, who was trying hard to look very small in her chair. I suspected that some of the party begrudged his argument and bravado, and even his wine.

A year later the couple's first child, a son, was born. I was godfather to the leg-kicking tyke. 'He's goin' to be a soccer player, Rami,' Cripes whispered to me. 'Look at him kick those legs.'

And no, he didn't name his son Cripes Junior, or Blimey, either. He named him Caesar Randall. What a man! He had made the great leap from reading Brad and Arlene's discarded books to dabbling in Ancient Roman History, God bless his soul.

Two years after Donna Rae graduated from Shortwood, I obtained my BA degree from UWI. My major in Geography was a good choice, too. On my return I learned that Mr Dumfries, who taught Geography at the High School, and who had helped me master my course in Advanced Geography, would be retiring in December. His position would be filled by the junior teacher under him, thus making the junior position open. It was mine to fill if I wanted it. Of course I wanted it. Things were falling into place. Robin Hill awaited me. Donna Rae awaited me.

I got the charred walls of Robin Hill knocked down. I intended to rebuild on the same spot, with a different architectural design, but one at least worthy of the first and, hopefully, better.

Cripes had done a magnificent job. The fields were looking good and producing abundantly. With the constant planting of young shoots, the banana fields both on my side of the river and on the other continued to march up the hill. The animals were doing fine and were healthy: three cows, two with calves and a heifer which I might decide to sell; and the goats were steadily producing kids. My bank account was getting fat. I was heady with triumph. The circle would soon be closed.

21

Full circle

Ma needed to move out of the rented house and build one of her own. I told her she should consider buying the strip of land that Mr Gregson had sold Father before he died. It had been Father's intention to build a store there. I had abandoned the idea of building the store so why should the land be left lying idle? I encouraged her to purchase the land and build a house on it. The frontage was not very wide, but the plot was deep, and a house built far from the street and on the mound would be well placed.

I knew she would have reservations, and she had. What would people say? They'd think she had divorced Sun-Sun, and now that he had died she was planning to live on his land, land he had bought after the divorce.

'You would've bought it, Ma,' I argued.

'Sure. But would they know?'

'You would. I would.'

'I don't know, Rami.'

'I'll put up a For Sale sign and make sure you're the first to make an offer.'

'I still don't like the idea.'

But she warmed to my proposal after I told her of my plans for Arlene and Brad. Money from the sale would be held in trust for them. Moreover I would let them have an income from the land I was farming. After all the land was our father's and, had he lived, he would have been providing for them. I also planned to have a will drawn up so that all three of us – Arlene, Brad and I – were named heirs.

Ma was astonished. 'You think of everything, don't you? Everything and everyone.' After a long pause she conceded. 'Okay, Rami, I'll do it.'

That was settled.

I don't think I could have hired a better man than Cripes. He was putting heart and soul into his stewardship. Of course he had the best of both worlds. He was not only the headman with a comfortable salary, but he had the free run of the properties and whatever they had to offer. He could take his share of the milk from the cows, whichever one had calved, and of the eggs from the hens. There was a cornucopia of food and fruits all around him, things with which he could feed his family. And he lived in a low-rent home. He was forever thankful to me for putting him on the road to success so he took a special interest in the farm.

Now that I was back in town I took the management of the finances back from Ma, and with my faith in Cripes growing steadily, I gave him more responsibilities. He was now being sent to the credit union with my withdrawal slip, retrieving the money, packaging it and paying the men and women who worked for him. Cripes was proud, his wife was prouder. Dressed in khaki and wearing a pith helmet, Cripes was reborn.

After a year of teaching I began to rebuild Robin Hill. With a good credit rating I had no trouble securing a mortgage and the contractor got things going.

I haven't said much about Donna Rae recently, have I? Well, as a teacher she was doing a swell job. She had returned from college armed with new ideas. At times she took her class out of the classroom and into the community. She took them on trips to the river where they studied river ecology, collecting specimens of crayfish, tadpoles and water beetles. Whenever it was appropriate, she involved members of the community in her lessons. She invited a local artist in to teach her pupils new techniques. In one instance she had them put on a play and got the parents involved by having them help to make costumes. Yes, as a teacher she was making her mark.

But so much for teaching.

We were not only dating; I had slipped a diamond ring on her finger. Ma had no objections. How could she? This juggernaut of love had bowled her over. No longer did she refer to Donna Rae as 'that girl'. It was Miss Hilcher to her face, and Donna Rae whenever she and I spoke of her future daughter-in-law.

Mrs Hilcher was proud of the development. She liked the match. I suspected she was already mentally designing the mother-of-all wedding dresses for her daughter and also tinkering in her head with the ingredients of the cake.

Not only did I get some old-fashioned ribbing from my sibs about my 'girlfriend' but I was peppered with questions.

'When is the big event, Rami?'

'After the "I do's" are you going to give her a tame kiss or plant a big wet one on her?'

'How many children do you two plan to have anyway?'

'Are you going to name any boy-baby Brad?'

'That's so stupid, Brad,' cracked Arlene. 'How many Brads can one family have?'

'A hundred! Even a zillion!'

At this point I took advantage and escaped because the two would continue to argue about who was stupider. Imps.

One Sunday in the square Donna Rae and I met the older Randalls and Cripes and his wife, the latter carrying baby Caesar. The younger Randalls were returning home from their church and the rest of us from the Anglican. We chit-chatted for a while until young Mrs Randall poked Cripes in the ribs.

'Oh yes,' began Cripes. He cleared his throat before he continued. '. . . Rami, I wonder . . . you know . . . er if you would . . . you know sell us the house. Down at River Bottom.'

For a moment or so I considered then I said, 'Cripes, I would gladly do so, but is it a good place for you and your wife and young family to live permanently? I think not. Down there you're cut off from everybody. You have no neighbours. Mrs Hilcher has left. And your children, Caesar here and those to follow him, will have no friends to play with while they're growing up. Tell you what I think,' I continued, switching my gaze to his father, 'a better idea would be to let your father give you a lot right here in the hub of town. He has a nice piece of land sitting just around the bend.' I made a flourish with my arm. 'It'd be a better environment for your family. Well, Mr Randall?'

I knew immediately I had made a mistake. Manny Randall was not only grinding his teeth but that sunshine smile that had landscaped his face a minute ago, had vanished. No one, and I mean no one, should tell Manny Randall what to do, and I had just attempted to. Even if he meant to do something anyway, if someone mentioned it first, it was curtains for that idea.

'Young Johnson, you got a good head on you shoulders.' That was all he said, neither yes or no to my suggestion. But I could see by the look on his face that the thought was going through his head: 'Who you think you are tellin' Manny Randall what to do?'

Two days later Cripes was smiling pure radiance. 'Pop said yes, Rami. He said I can have the lot.' He shook my hand. 'Thank you. You're the first man I know who told Pop what to do and he done it.'

'Of course, Cripes, you may stay at River Bottom for as long as you wish. That way you can save money to build your dream home.'

'Right,' he said. 'That's a good idea.'

The house at Robin Hill was up, the roof tiled red, and workmen were plastering the outer walls, while inside others were installing the plumbing and light fixtures, cupboards and such. Since Donna Rae would be mistress of the house, she had had equal input not only in the house's design but in the fixtures, paint colours and other details.

Ma's house was coming along nicely, as well. It had three bedrooms and a verandah that wrapped around three sides of it.

Donna Rae and I bucked the trend and got married in March instead of the favourite month of June. And why wait? We were ready. Robin Hill awaited us. We were twenty-three. Donna Rae had no sisters or close relatives who fitted the age group so Arlene stood in as flower girl; four bridesmaids, all dressed in lilac, completed the party.

My bride was singularly stunning. She wore a sheath gown of white lace with a satin overskirt appliquéd with lace. The bodice of lace had a midriff of pleated satin and boasted a Sabrina neckline. Her headdress was a coronet of crystals and pearls from which fell a shoulder-length veil of illusion tulle. She carried a bouquet of white gladiola and camellias. I loved what I saw.

Mrs Hilcher had outdone herself this time, and why not? Donna Rae was her only daughter, only child. She wouldn't have another chance to dress her again for a wedding. I'd make sure of that. My best man was my best friend, Collie Rainer.

I won't go into details of the reception that followed the ceremony, other than to remark that Manny Randall had no need to float any objections, because this wedding, like the one at Cana of Galilee and many others after it, boasted wine. Of course there was fruit punch, too, for those whose religion prevented them from indulging in strong drink. However, I will mention one other person – Cripes. He was not the only one who toasted me, but his toast was special because of the academic road he had travelled. I was amazed at the words that tumbled from his mouth.

'I'd like to propose a toast to the bridegroom, my boss, and I quote the poet, Longfellow:

> The heights by great men reached and kept
> Were not attained by sudden flight
> But they, while their companions slept,
> Were toiling upwards in the night.

To the bridegroom.' He raised his glass of fruit punch and everybody drank.

Where had he come across that poem? My bride whispered an explanation. Cripes had found the poem lying on the street, apparently ripped from a student's poetry book. He liked that particular verse so much he went to Donna Rae for her opinion. Was it appropriate as a toast? She gave it her blessing so Cripes had memorized it.

When he got me aside he said, 'Rami, I think that verse was written just for you. It said everything you've done.'

'Thank you, Cripes. But you know', I complimented him, 'it applies to you as well as to me.'

'You think so?' he grinned.

'You know it's so, Cripes. You took flight and you've touched the sky.'

Donna Rae had her flourish of toasts too, more than I. From school friends, from her principal and fellow teachers, and from her uncle, who had given her away, and also from the Rev. Ledbetter.

One last tidbit before this chapter is closed. Donna Rae and I are now twenty-four and the first member of the Rami and Donna Rae Johnson family is on the way.